the MAGIC CIRCLE

DONNA JO NAPOLI

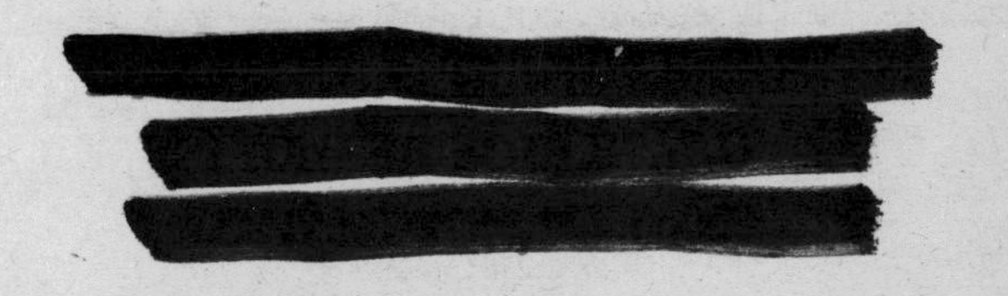

PUFFIN BOOKS

PUFFIN BOOKS
Published by the Penguin Group
Penguin Books USA Inc., 375 Hudson Street, New York, New York 10014, U.S.A.
Penguin Books Ltd, 27 Wrights Lane, London W8 5TZ, England
Penguin Books Australia Ltd, Ringwood, Victoria, Australia
Penguin Books Canada Ltd, 10 Alcorn Avenue, Toronto, Ontario, Canada M4V 3B2
Penguin Books (N.Z.) Ltd, 182-190 Wairau Road, Auckland 10, New Zealand

Penguin Books Ltd, Registered Offices: Harmondsworth, Middlesex, England

First published in the United States of America by Dutton Children's Books,
a division of Penguin Books USA Inc., 1993
Published in Puffin Books, 1995

3 5 7 9 10 8 6 4

THE LIBRARY OF CONGRESS HAS CATALOGED THE DUTTON EDITION AS FOLLOWS:
Napoli, Donna Jo.
The magic circle / by Donna Jo Napoli.—1st ed. p. cm.
Summary: After learning sorcery to become a healer, a good-hearted woman
is turned into a witch by evil spirits, and she fights their power
until her encounter with Hansel and Gretel years later.
ISBN 0-525-45127-7
[1. Fairy tales. 2. Witches—Fiction.] I. Title.
PZ8.[illegible]127Mag 1993 [F[illegible]]—dc20 [illegible]2-27008 CIP AC

Puffin Books ISBN 0-14-037439-6

Printed in Canada

For Lucia Monfried, who told me, "Just write it down."
With a sea of gratitude.

CONTENTS

I thank the following people for their comments on an earlier draft: Barry Furrow, Curt Kallas, Stephen Lehmann, Bob Schachner, Judy Schachner, Don Swearer, Nancy Swearer, Chuck Tilly, Louise Tilly, Eric van der Vlugt, and Gill van der Vlugt. All of them kept me from making errors of history, culture, and geography. Errors that remain are evidence of my own stubbornness.

one

The Journey Begins

Summer comes over the hill like a hairy blanket. Asa rolls onto her side, and her light brown hair falls away from her pink cheek. Her coloring gives evidence of the north country of her grandmother, dead now many years. Her nose twitches, rabbitlike, as though she realizes, even in her sleep, that the warm weather is finally here. I run my fingertips across the fine fuzz of hair on her temple.

"Ahhh," says Asa. "Good morning, Mother."

The air around us is calm. I do not want to disturb it by rising. Instead, I reach over to the basket in the corner near our bed. "Look," I say, holding up the treasure.

Asa opens her mouth in awe. The amber ribbon

matches the highlights in her hair. She plucks it from my hand eagerly. "Where did you get it?"

"Tzipi gave it to me, for birthing her."

"You shouldn't take a ribbon," says Asa. "You should take something we need. You should take wool." Her actions don't match her words. She is brushing the silky ribbon against her cheek.

Her words are grown-up for her age. I don't marvel at that fact, and I don't fight the inevitable. Poor children are always more grown-up in that way. But I am gladdened that she can hold the ribbon against her cheek and allow herself to want it. "It's summer," I say, "summer at last. I'll take wool when it's closer to autumn." I smile. "For now, you have a ribbon for your hair."

Asa wraps the ribbon around her fingers. "It's beautiful, Mother."

"No more beautiful than you."

I weave the ribbon into Asa's hair, and she runs from the cabin to show the world.

Before I have time to finish straightening our things, a neighbor bursts in upon me. It is Bala. "Ugly One," she says to me, "have you no sense at all? You trade your midwifery skills for a ribbon?"

"More than a ribbon," I say. "For beauty."

"Tzipi is seducing you with her non-Christian ways," says Bala.

I laugh away her hatred of the outsider, grateful my mother taught me this use of mirth. "Beauty is not dangerous to those who truly love God. It is a joy, Bala. I must have it in my home."

"For Asa," says Bala, finishing with the very words that were on the tip of my tongue.

"She deserves emeralds," I say, "rubies, even gold." I smile at the thought. "Oh, decorative visions." I wave my hands at the walls around our small room. I breathe deeply of the woody air. These walls are covered with wreaths made from tiny spruce cones with dried gooseberries and holly berries attached with balsam fir resin. A collection of colored feathers overflows a clay bowl on the floor. In a dish nearby are thin slices of mica. I pick one up now and hold it to the window. The sunbeam breaks into colors that dance on my arm.

Bala sighs. "How did such an ugly one as you get such an eye for beauty?"

That question is easily answered. I have only to think of my mother's hair, always arranged this way or that to show the fine line of her jaw. She was too poor to have ribbons. But she had wildflowers in her hair. Purple heather and golden gorse. I could tell Bala this. But I don't. It is not good to remind Bala that I have different blood in me. It has taken many years to find my place in this village. I fit now.

Bala moves closer and whispers. "How did such an ugly one as you have such a beautiful daughter?"

Now I remain silent because I have no answer. I have asked myself that question many times. My mind touches briefly on Asa's father, the one my memory has named the Patient Scholar, the one who opened for me the world of letters. I see his face, square and plain, gray—not beautiful to anyone's eyes but mine. I can almost touch it in my memory. I have not visited him since my belly first became round with Asa. For an instant I almost believe I can know that he lives still, that he thinks rarely and briefly of me, alone in his scholar's world. Steeped in the perfection of his mind and soul, he is unaware of his offspring.

"Tell me," comes Bala's insistent whisper, now raspy. "He glows in your eyes. Tell me about him."

I give the answer I always give: "It is best not to speak of the dead." The words are no lie. They do not say he is dead to this world—only to me. That the villagers accept this answer and keep me in their fold is, likewise, no miracle. They need a midwife. It is only Bala who receives my answer without gratitude, without relief. She has not moved since I spoke. She is too close. I pronounce each word with resonance: "It is best to let the dead go."

Bala looks at me sharply all of a sudden. "Did you know that Otto of the West Forest is looking for a midwife? His wife has lost three babies already. He says he'll pay anything for a midwife who can make this baby live."

Payment from a noble would not be a single bale of wool or a lone ribbon. I cannot begin to imagine what it would be. I cannot begin to imagine what I might want it to be. Confusion floods me. I am unaccustomed to this sort of speculation. I am disturbed by the tiny flicker of curiosity and want. I replace the mica in the dish and scrape a wart off my elbow, hoping Bala does not read the mixed emotions in my face. "Otto of the West Forest would not take an ugly midwife."

"He would if he knew your reputation," says Bala. "You've saved the smallest newborns. You've nursed back to health the sickest mothers. Your hands are deft." She takes my hands and turns them so the palms are open to her. "These hands read a pregnant belly and fly to the task. You have the gift of birthing."

I pull my hands back, surprised by the praise. Bala has never before shown such interest in me. "God is good to me," I say.

The neighbor Bala cocks her head. "I'll tell this desperate noble of you. I'll have him begging for you. But then you must give me part of what he pays you."

I nod.

Bala rushes out, her greed cleaving the air.

I put Bala and her needs and Otto of the West Forest and his needs out of my mind. The day is long and hot and lazy. Asa spends most of it in the stream, then the meadow, then the stream again.

I feel almost without worry. The summer will be long. Food will be plentiful. I let myself slide inside my head, down and around, faster and faster, into God's waiting hands. I am ready for those hands to close over me, to envelop me in the love that has no bounds. But today the hands sit open. Something is uneven, off balance. There is something I must learn. But I feel stupid today. I've been too lazy all day. I cannot learn what God wants me to learn.

"Ugly One!"

Bala's scream jerks me back to the world where mortals walk. I stand up to meet her. Even standing as tall as I can, I am stooped over so much my nose reaches only to her shoulder.

She looks at my twisted back for a second. "Oh," says

Bala, "they will have a shock when they see you. But Otto of the West Forest is waiting. You must hurry."

"Asa," I call.

Asa runs to me.

We walk to the noble's house, past the well-tended fields, toward the dark cool of the small woodland. It takes us most of an hour. Bala explains to Asa what lies ahead of us. Asa is eager. She has seen many peasant babies born. But this is the first time she will see a noble's home from the inside. It is my first time, as well. I stay silent, trying to roll in God's hands, trying to understand what it is I'm supposed to learn today. Is there something I must know to save the noble's baby?

And then Asa is sitting with Otto of the West Forest, with the noble himself, and, lo, she is even singing in her trill of a voice, though no one listens. Bala is pacing outside the door, and I am alone with the noble's wife. Her eyes are sunk in her fat face. My heart goes out to her fear. She clutches at my cloak. On her hand is a ring of orange and yellow golds from Spain. Bala spoke of the Spanish gold in this house as we walked here, but her description did not prepare me for the splendor. The ring's face is a large, raised oval with a figure eight in the middle. Around the eight are grape leaves with clusters of grapes. It is as near to perfect a ring as I can imagine.

The wife's grasp is so strong, I almost lose my balance. I rub her thighs hard. Already I know the presentation is wrong. But it is early enough; the baby is not yet in the birth canal. I pull a clean new leather strap from the folds of my cloak and hand it to the frantic woman. She knows to hold it in her teeth and scream and bite. I reach inside her with one hand, and with the other I work the outside of her belly. The child must be turned. I have a baby shoulder under my palm. I massage the small lump downward. I push and work and the wife screams.

It is night as the baby gasps for air. A girl. I suck the mucus from her nose and place her naked and wet at her mother's breast. The girl baby suckles, and I laugh. The new mother laughs and cries and laughs. We feel lucky to have shared a miracle. For this one moment we are as sisters, overflowing with love. Ephemeral bond. But she is tired. I back out of the room.

Bala has been sent home. Asa is asleep in the barn. I go to her and lie beside her. Tomorrow, Otto of the West Forest has promised, tomorrow I may choose my payment. I fall asleep thinking of Spanish gold. Orange and yellow gold.

The gold of morning sun on straw wakens me. Mosquitoes have already begun to plague the barn. I snap my hands in the air, keeping them from Asa's face. Then we are called to the house.

The noble has a pouch of money hanging from his wrist. He holds it out for me to feel its weight. "Money for a job well-done. Or, perhaps, something else?" He extends a closed fist. "I've heard of your love of beautiful things." He opens his fist. An emerald glistens at me.

I look at Asa. Her eyes are on the table in the room beyond. I follow her gaze. The table is laden with fruits and nuts in large porcelain bowls. I shake my head. "Asa, look at the emerald."

"Candy, Mother." Asa walks to the table and the noble follows her. "There are mints and chocolates," she says.

Otto of the West Forest laughs. He places a square of chocolate in Asa's mouth, almost as the local pastor would place the host in our waiting mouths. He hands her a circle of green mint. He looks at me. "Have you decided?"

"The emerald," I hear myself saying.

When we get home, Bala is waiting on the dirt path. "An emerald?" she screams. "How am I to take a part of an emerald? You must trade it immediately for clothes and food."

I search the land, the trees, the skies with my eyes. "What can I set the emerald in for Asa to wear?"

"You fool!" screams Bala. "If she wears an emerald, she'll be robbed. Robbed. And maybe killed, too."

Bala is right. The emerald must be hidden. We must find a treasure hole. Bala talks on and on, but my mind is already peering into every hole I know, looking for the right one, when my eyes finally pass the door of our cabin. Above the door is the green circle of mint. Asa has climbed up onto the roof to place it there.

Asa smiles at us from the roof. "Don't you love it, Mother? We can know it is there. We can shut our eyes and pretend we live in a candy house. All candy. Everywhere."

"The birds will eat it," screams Bala. It seems she can do nothing but scream this day.

"I lacquered it," says Asa. She slides off the roof and runs toward the stream. She is much smarter than the ordinary five-year-old. I can feel Bala's anger following Asa's back.

"Birds won't eat a lacquered mint," I say to Bala, relishing Asa's victory over the logic of Bala—the logic of these hard and ascetic people.

"Shut up, Ugly One," she says. "I did you a favor. You owe me now."

"Yes," I say, stifling my smile. "The next birthing I do, the payment goes to you."

"No. Midwifery around here brings nothing more than sacks of flour or bales of wool. And none of the other nobles' wives are heavy with child." Bala sighs. Then she says slowly, "But the burgermeister's first child is ill."

I am silent. There is nothing to say.

"You can cure him." Bala looks at me with bird eyes. "You."

"I am a simple midwife," I say. "I am not a healer."

"You could be. You know the secrets of nature better than anyone. You bring down milk fever in new mothers. You banish the pus from newborns' eyes." Bala dances around me as she talks. "Why, you are a healer already. Everyone is astonished at what you know—at what you can do."

"Devils bring illness. Only those who can chase devils away can heal."

"You are a woman of God," says Bala. "You can chase devils away."

I shake my head, not daring to allow the conversation to go any further. "Not me," I say, but already the stirrings of new hope are alive within me. No one has ever asked me to step beyond the limits of the birthing bed.

"How can a woman of God say such a thing?" Bala puts her face close to mine. "Every God-fearing soul battles with devils daily."

"There is a difference," I say, my heart beating faster, "between fighting devils in the daily battle of souls and seeking out devils for a battle of choice."

Bala squats on the ground and looks hard at the dirt. She picks up a stick and draws a large circle. "But if you could chase devils away without endangering yourself, you would do it, wouldn't you?"

I think of the plains stretching to the north, crisscrossed with streams. My mother and I walked there. She pointed out the herbs. She showed me the medicinal value of the hare's liver. She revealed to me the secrets of the river fish. I know cures from her. And through the years I have added my own. I have experimented, always following my instinct. But until now my cures have been offered only to newborns and their mothers and to my own sweet Asa. My heart is now in my throat. My breath comes hard. "I would heal if I could."

"Then we must make you a magic circle," says Bala. "You can stay entirely within the magic circle, and no devil can get you."

"A magic circle," I whisper. This is what God wanted me to learn yesterday. I am sure. I will learn from Bala.

She is an unexpected wealth of knowledge. I must learn about this magic circle.

"Yes," says Bala. "You will be paid by everyone." She pauses for effect. She believes I want the worldly pay. Maybe she believes I want to build a house of emeralds. "You will be paid well." Her voice is avarice itself. "And I will take my share. You will be our holy one to drive away devils." She smiles.

I roll in God's hand and feel fingers closing gently over me. Instantly, I know; this is it. This is why I was put on this earth. This is my calling.

Bala says in a strong voice, "You will be God's helper. Our own village sorceress."

And thus begins the dangerous journey.

two

The Magic Circle

I sit by the stream where it burbles the loudest. No one else must hear me. I practice the syllables, starting at the end of the word: "Cajfz." It is difficult to train my tongue. How can a syllable end with so many sounds? I practice over and over, until the syllable feels solid. Then I add another syllable. My lips can't seem to move fast enough. I work and work. Only a true sorcerer can pronounce the unspeakable word. And only perfect pronunciation commands a devil. I must keep working. I add a third syllable, always tacking onto the beginning. It's getting easier. Lips and tongue and teeth are all cooperating now. I let it grow. But I cannot add the first syllable. If I say the full word, I will call the demons, and I must not call them until I am ready to face them. That will be when I am safely within the magic circle. Bala has gathered information from sources I must not ask about. She has assured me it will all go well, once I am within the magic circle. I take a deep breath now and repeat the incomplete word: "Diatmoaamvpmsciccajfz."

The word makes me smile. I realize now why I practiced from the end to the front. The front of the word is easy. Fools are lured into thinking they see simplicity. Then they stumble on the final sounds, and devils laugh at them. Bala tells me if the devils laugh loud enough, fools have been known to rush from the magic circle to a most hideous fate. Since I have no experience with these things, I listen to her and to all who tell of devils. I record each detail. Who knows what may be useful some day?

Fools race over the sacred word and thus seal their own fate. But those who start at the end learn to appreciate the difficulty. They never forget whose presence they are in.

I will speak the unspeakable. Yes. I will call devils unto me by saying correctly the words they must obey. The devils will not laugh at me. And I will never forget their power.

As I sit here, my thoughts are in harmony with my

actions. The care with which I perform each action is crucial. Recognition and respect, these form the foundations of sorcery. My performance must be meticulous, so that God and devils sense my recognition of and respect for their powers. I rise thoughtfully, my head full of anticipation of the first meeting that lies ahead.

The first meeting with the devils is the most dangerous. On the first meeting I do not know which devil it is that inhabits the sick child's body. I will not yet have even seen the child. At that meeting I am forced to call all devils at once. I am in the most grave danger that I will ever be in. But so long as I stay entirely within the magic circle, so long as no part of me, no wisp of hair, no curl of breath, extends beyond the circle, the devils cannot get to me.

The magic circle. The limit of my humble abilities.

I leave the stream and walk to the cabin, buffered by a fog of vague worry, distanced from the fine edges of things of this world. The magic circle.

"Get that look off your face," says Bala in her crow voice. Her beady eyes hold me fast. In her hands is the sword she told me she would steal. "You'll worry the burgermeister if you enter his house with that sick look."

"How can I not have a sick look?" My own worry sharpens now. Bala's methods disturb me. I have worked the night and the morning to suppress my fear. But it will not be quelled. Bala is wrong. I point accusingly at the blade. "I will not touch that sword."

"You must touch the sword," says Bala. "Without it, you cannot draw the magic circle."

"I can use anything to draw the circle," I say, "anything blessed."

"And what have you got that is blessed?" says Bala.

I have no answer.

"No dean of any cathedral, Protestant or Catholic, near or far, would bless something for a hunchback like you."

I look at Bala in silence.

She makes a *tsk*ing noise. "The sword belongs to our own pastor. It is blessed."

"And stolen," I say.

Bala moves close to me. "He would never lend it to you, a woman, an ugly hunchback. I had no choice. I'll give it back when you've finished." Her wet breath stings my cheek like the acid orange and yellow fruits from the south.

"When I've finished, if the boy is well," I say, stepping away, "there will be another healing job. And then another. And you will never return the sword."

"Wretched Ugly One," screams Bala.

"I must be pure of heart, or no magic circle can stave

off the devils. If I use a stolen sword, how can I be pure of heart?"

"You didn't steal it," says Bala. "I stole it. You are pure. I am not."

"But I know it is stolen," I say. "It's no use, Bala."

"You think too much," screams Bala.

"And you think too little," I say.

"Mother." Asa comes from inside the cabin. She holds a fish wrapped in wide oak leaves. The tail gleams. She peels a leaf from its head. The twisted face of the plaice fish, with both eyes on its right side, gleams like the moon I believe my child has sprung from. "A plaice fish is sacred, Mother. A plaice fish is blessed."

I shut my eyes and see the plaice fish swimming, flattened against the bottom of the distant North Sea, twisted like me. How did Asa get this fish? How could a five-year-old get such a fish? Must I ask? Asa has a smile like my mother's. She could easily charm a fisherman into giving her this fish. Besides, few people eat plaice. It would be worth nothing to the fisherman. "Skin it, Asa. You do it. Cut away its flesh. But leave the tail and backbone and head intact."

"No!" Bala hovers over the fish. "See how fat it is?" Her words are true. The fish is fatter than any plaice fish I have ever seen before. "Come." Bala takes my hand

and places it on the fish's belly. "Feel the motion, Midwife." She looks at me with cold eyes. "You can guess as well as I." Her hand squeezes mine. "A slime eel."

My breath catches. As a child, I lived by the sea. I am no stranger to its horrors. I imagine the plaice's inner cavity slick with slime, host to the gray, writhing hideous eel.

I search Bala's eyes. I have never talked to her of my childhood. We have never discussed the hated slime eels. Yet I have the sense that she knows the effect her guess has upon me. Slowly I move my eyes from Bala's stone face to the clear, hopeful eyes of my child. Asa questions me with those eyes. She makes no guesses. She trusts me. I move my fingers along the scales, polished smooth by the rocks of the seafloor. To my hand the belly is quiet. To my hand this fish is clean. It is good. I know this is a moment, one of the many moments to come, when I must trust my own judgment as much as Asa does.

"Bring the knife here, Asa. Prepare the fish in front of us."

Asa smiles. She does not know what a slime eel is. She is merely glad to see her fish has pleased me, after all. She sets it on the ground and runs to the cabin. Bala follows her and stands at the threshold. Asa returns moments later with the knife. She slits the fish neatly from anus to mouth and peels it from the bone. The soft globose innards fall in the dirt.

Bala stands on the doorstep and watches. Her eyes are angry. Pride is a heavy burden.

I meet her eyes without triumph. There is no need to kindle the flame. Bala is my friend, after all. "Return the sword," I say gently.

She lifts her chin and glides away toward her cabin. She has a fluidity of motion my body has never known.

Within the hour I am walking off to the birch grove. Asa and Bala have promised not to follow. I can take no chances with the souls of others. Bala has whispered my intent to others. One villager told me to bring parchment and use a quill to write the devils' names in my own blood on the parchment. But I have no parchment. Another told me to bring the hide of a freshly killed goat and write upon it. But where would I get such a hide? I have tasted no meat except squirrel since the last winter solstice. My handwriting is in any case unlovely, even if blood makes it divine. The written word is only as powerful as the scribe is talented. And Bala has reassured me that none of these things is necessary. I go empty-handed, but for the plaice fish.

Still I feel the need to spill my own blood. It is a sacrifice of sorts—a gift to God as I ask for protection. I unwrap the fish head and spine. There are many sharp bones. I snap one off and pierce my calf, drawing a line from the inside of my knee to my ankle. A thin red rivulet races to the dry ground.

My shoes are brown, as is my cloak. It is the only cloak I have. I take off both shoes and cloak and stand in my white shift. Sorcerers should be dressed in white linen robes spun by pure young maidens. I wonder if most sorcerers are wealthy. But if one was wealthy, why would one dare to converse with devils? Only desperation could make anyone draw a magic circle. Today, here among the white trunks of these straight trees, I am desperate.

And I wonder at my own desperation. I am desperate for beauty. I am overcome with the desperate desire to surround sweet Asa with jewels. To give her something as lovely as the gold ring of the wife of Otto of the West Forest. I laugh—jewels and candy. But that is not the desperation that draws me here now. The burgermeister's child suffers. I will help this child. I must. I must free him of illness so he can savor candy, just as Asa savored the chocolate put on her tongue by Otto of the West Forest. I must see the pleasure in the child's eyes as health returns. This will be my reward for meeting with the devils. I laugh again.

I cannot stop laughing.

But finally, I am weakened. The tears wet my cheeks. I put the fish head to the ground and walk backward in a circle, dragging it. The magic circle is faint, but it forms undeniably. There is but a thumb's length left to close it. I make sure I am within the incomplete circle. I press my hair flat to my head. I rub my forearms. Then I pick up the fish head and complete the circle. I am now enveloped.

I sit in the center and fold my legs across each other. The rivulet on my calf has dried. I have no idea how long it takes to summon the devils. I have no grimoire, no magic textbook. I have only my purity of soul and my one magic word, the word that calls all demons. The villagers have told me that I will see horrible sights. Everyone seems to be an expert on devils. Everyone but me. Nevertheless, I know I am prepared. I whisper. "Adiatmoaamvpmsciccajfz."

I expect to whisper many times. But before my tongue can relax from the sibilance of the final *z*, a face appears before me. It is a beautiful face. The face of a small child. I know not whether the child is male or female.

The child smiles at me. "Mother."

I feel the urge to hold this child. How did a child come to be in these woods at this hour? Why was I so foolish as to not search the area first to make sure there were no intruders? The child must have been behind the closest birch, but three feet away. I should have checked there. I should have checked everywhere. Now this child is in danger. I want to hold the child. I need to hold the child. Against every desire I have, I say, "Run, child. Run away quickly. The devils come."

The child looks hurt. "Mother."

Where is this child's mother? "I am not your mother."

"Mother," says the child in a trusting voice.

I cannot shoo the child away again. I must hold the child. Suddenly I realize that if I call the child into the magic circle, the child cannot be harmed. "Come here, child. Hurry." I stretch out my hands. They reach almost to the edge of the circle. I am giddy with the knowledge that the child will be safe if we are both within the magic circle.

The child lifts the tiny robe it wears, to show feet covered with blood. "Come, Mother."

I gasp at the wounded feet. This child cannot come to me. I must go to the child. I stand up and look about carefully. Are there devils hiding in the woods? "Reach out your hands, child. Reach to me."

The child reaches, but the small pudgy hands do not extend into the magic circle. I must take the risk and grab the child swiftly, clasp the child to me before the avenging devils appear. I stand up shakily. Then the cold doubt hits me. What if this child is a trick? A devil in disguise. Is that possible? I look at the child.

The child falls toward me and looks up with huge eyes. "Mother, help." There is blood on the child's cheek. I have been told demons do not bleed. This is common wisdom. If only I could taste the blood, know if it was true.

But even from here I can see it is true blood. It is red and thick and it gives off a sweet odor. I must save this child. It is up to me. I take a step. Another. I am blinded by fear. And in my blindness I step on the fish spine. A bone pierces my foot. The pain shoots up me like a raging fire. I stumble, and a drop of my blood flies out of the circle. I hear the sound of steam as my blood hits the child's face.

A horned skeleton leers at me, teeth black and pointed. I know those teeth are iron. "Almost, Ugly One. We almost got you."

The fire within me turns to ice. I shake with the realization that I almost perished. I am not a match for the treachery of the devil. There is no child. There never was one.

"What is it, Ugly One? Why do you summon us?"

I look around. There is only one devil, but he speaks of "us." I listen to the rustling all about. The woods must be filled with evil. "Who inhabits the body of the child of the burgermeister?"

My question is direct. The demon must answer. "Astaroth, the smelly one."

"When I am with the burgermeister," I say, "I will call forth Astaroth and banish him from the child's body. And he will leave forever."

The devil swings a pointed tail close to the circle, closer and closer. "A visit in the damp and dark will serve much better than the lark." He laughs.

I kiss the plaice fish head. "God be with you."

The devil shrivels and is gone.

The air smells faintly of silver nitrate. I recognize it from the north country Festival of Lights my mother took me to as a girl. I wrap the fish head and spine and tail in the oak leaves again and prepare to step from the circle. But the mark of the circle is gone.

I need it no longer.

I have met the devil and survived. Were I a Catholic priest, I would now be an exorcist. But I am only a peasant woman. I am a sorceress. The Ugly Sorceress.

three

Healing

I repeat the words of the devil: "A visit in the damp and dark will serve much better than the lark." A devil may not lie to a sorcerer. Devils are obedient servants. Yet every instinct I have tells me that I must not call Astaroth in the damp and dark. The lark is the bird of the dawn. The plaice fish migrates southward, toward the sunny lands. I must summon Astaroth on a sunny day, before the shadows of late afternoon. I know this, without knowing how I know. But the devil's words confound me. Why does he advise me to call Astaroth at the wrong time? I repeat the words slowly: "A visit in the damp and dark will serve much better than the lark." And now

I am smiling. Serve, yes, that is the key. Such a visit would serve better—but whom would it serve? The devil, of course. Astaroth would never hasten to my summons in the damp and dark. This devil craves brightness. My instincts are right. I must go tomorrow morning if it is hot and sunny. I must go when the lark would sing.

And dawn comes finally, to my eyes that have held no sleep. It comes wavering through the heat that rises off the summer earth.

"Asa," I call from the step.

"Yes, Mother," calls Asa from her niche in the cedar tree. She climbs like a tree-dweller, while I get dizzy at the very thought of heights.

"What birds have you seen this morning?" I say.

"Only the sparrows, Mother."

I wring my hands. "What birds have you heard this morning?"

"Only the lark, Mother."

"Ahh," I say with relief. "I am going to the burgermeister's house. Come, Asa."

We walk in our customary silence. Halfway across the deep green meadow, Bala joins us. She, too, stays silent. But for her the silence is uncustomary. I think of the fears Asa and Bala must have. Yet today I have no fear. I have met with a devil. Perhaps with many devils. I will not be fooled by any bleeding child. I will be fooled by nothing.

We arrive at the burgermeister's home after a much longer walk than I expected. I am tired, though the ground was flat. The burgermeister leads us to the boy's bedroom with no pretenses at niceties.

The boy is thin and pale. His corneas are yellow. There is a crust of drool on his chin. His bedclothes smell fetid. I don't need to touch his skin to feel the heat that emanates from him. His bed is on a platform in the center of the room. On a tray at the foot of the bed sit a bowl of clear broth and a rigid reed the boy must use to suck up the broth. It is good that someone knows enough to keep him from dehydrating. I walk around the bed, making sure the path is clear.

I realize suddenly that I have not brought the plaice fish. I spin around and face the burgermeister. "Bring me . . ." I am about to speak of his sword, but I catch myself in time. The burgermeister is the financial officer of this region, but he rose from a humble source. He may not have a noble's sword. I must not shame him. "Have you anything blessed?"

The man looks frightened. "My sword."

Relief fills me, but the frightened man's face is unchanged, of course. He does not know his answer is the best it could be. I wonder where he has banished his wife. He would be embarrassed to show such fear in front of her. "It will be of use," I say. He hesitates still. "Because it is blessed," I add to comfort him.

He leaves and returns with the sword. The hilt is bedecked with amethysts. Asa was born in February, like my mother, whom she is named after. The amethyst is her stone. It is a good sign. And the amethyst wards off drunkenness. I have never been drunk. Yet I know power can make one drunk. The very thought of having the power to heal the child threatens to sodden me like beer. I feel tipsy. Giddy. Yes. I am in need of the amethyst. Oh, yes. It will keep my vision clear. I accept the heavy sword and know that God is pleased.

"Take everyone from this house," I say. I look meaningfully at Asa and Bala, who still stand behind the burgermeister. I turn back to the man. "Sit in the shade near water. In the damp and dark." I know I am using the devil's words against him. I know that Astaroth will not go near the burgermeister's family, will not go near Asa and Bala, if they stay in the damp and dark. I feel proud of myself for being so shrewd. Then I quickly repent of my pride. It is God's shrewdness, not my own, that speaks from my lips. I touch the amethysts of the sword in gratitude and say in a more gentle tone, "I will call you."

The burgermeister opens his mouth, but the protest doesn't come out. I can see the fear that makes his skin clammy. I look past him.

The walls of this room are covered with maps. But not just maps of the locality. Not just the lands the burgermeister collects taxes from. Also distant lands—with mountains and lakes whose names I have never heard before. I am surprised. A table stands near one wall with a large book open upon it. The burgermeister has earned his post: He is both a cartographer of sorts and a scholar, to at least a small degree.

I look again at his eyes. They are not now the calm eyes of a man of letters. He is discombobulated by the very fact that he has summoned a sorceress. He thinks I am a lunatic. But he is willing to talk with lunatics if his son will be saved. I can see how much he wants to save his son. I can feel his parched throat. I can hear his banging heart. I almost tell him that he doesn't need me. He wants to save his son so badly that he could call the devils himself. He doesn't need a sorcerer. Anyone can tame the devils if their want is strong enough. But this burgermeister would have to enter into a pact with the devils if he were to call them on his own. I do not. I am in league with God. It is my purity that empowers me. The man does need me, after all.

"Go," I command. This poor man needs to be ordered. He is beyond judgment and reason. "Go!"

When we are alone, the boy pulls a wooden boat out from under the bedclothes. He moves it across the coverlet in jerky spasms. He makes it rise and fall, cresting the unseen waves. I think of the boat I crossed the North Sea in with my mother so many years ago. I put the sword down carefully on the floor and watch the little boat's progress. The boy speaks without taking his eyes from the boat. "Are you a witch?"

His question is guileless and vulnerable. I am in awe of the control he must exercise to keep himself from screaming if he thinks he is in the presence of a witch. "A witch works for the devils." I smile kindly. "I am a sorceress—the devils work for me."

The boy's face shows no emotion, no relief at my words. He makes his toy boat founder in the waves of the coverlet. His hands fly around the distressed vessel as if the crew were jumping helter-skelter into the cold sea. Excitement brings color to his cheeks. His fingers are long and thin. His hands seem skeletal. Suddenly he rights the boat and looks up at me. I see the face of the angel he will become. He opens his mouth to speak. I lean forward to learn his secret. He says, "What is your name?"

A simple question. One any child might ask of any person. The wind of death has transfigured this boy's body, but inside he is still human, after all. Inside he is still a boy who plays with a toy boat. "They call me the Ugly Sorceress. What is yours?"

"Peter."

"Peter." I smile at the ordinariness of this boy's name. I had expected Hogarth or Hubert. A grand name, befitting the son of our chief elected official. I press my lips together and hesitate before the plunge. Then I dare to say the words I have practiced silently. "I'll heal you, Peter."

"You can't heal me." The boy's words are without self-pity. He tucks his boat under the covers and settles back onto his pillows. His face becomes placid. He looks like a miniature man. Almost wizened. "But if you can make me die swiftly," he says, "without pain, then I won't object to my father's paying you."

I move closer to the bed, drawn by the hopeless words. It is wrong for one so young to feel alone. It is wrong for anyone to be hopeless. Hopelessness is the bedchamber of the demons. I ache with the need to restore this child's faith. "Why do you say I can't heal you, Peter?"

"You are a hunchback. If you could heal, you would heal yourself."

I shake my head at his logic. I can see the burgermeister's discipline in his son. "It is my hump that has made me special all my life. It is God's mark on me. I carry it willingly."

"Then is not this disease I carry also God's mark?"

"No," I say. "It is the work of a devil that inhabits you."

"And how do you know?" says Peter, levelly. His fever-ravaged lips split at the quick movements of speech. "Just how do you know the difference? How can you tell what is the work of God and what is the work of the devils?"

"You aren't the child I expected," I say, feeling that if I let my hands loose, one from the other, they will flutter and fly away. There is a corner of a book sticking out from under the boy's pillows. The edges of the pages are dark and worn. As I look at this book, I realize Peter reads. Yes. He has the logic of one who reads. Not haltingly, as a schoolboy, but with hunger and facility. I am sure words on pages orient Peter's life. I am absolutely sure of this. I want to reorient him now. I want to waken the child inside, the child that pushed the boat across the imaginary waves just moments ago. I want him to have a child's innocent hope as we face our fates together. "What is the book, Peter?"

"This one?" Peter taps the corner of the book but doesn't pull it out. "I read all the time. My father's men search for books for me. Sometimes they are gone a whole week, they travel such distances." His fingers feel the leather of the book cover. They caress. His eyes stay on me. "This is a storybook of a special land, where wolves eat grandmothers." He stops for effect. I am encouraged. It is good that he wants me to care. I try to look properly impressed. He licks his split lip. "And young beggar girls get to be princesses for a night." His voice is almost happy, though it lacks timbre. I know from the quality of his voice that his chest is full of infection. I nod. Peter talks more. His dull eyes would shine if they could. "There are enchanted forests where humans dare not tread."

"A strange mixture," I say.

"A wonderful mixture. Beautiful girls run away from wicked stepmothers and talk to animals and ride on deers' backs and . . . oh." His face is wistful. "I would like to ride on a deer's back."

The child within is awake again. I can proceed. "Where is this land?" I ask, though my mind is no longer on this conversation. My mind struggles now with other questions, with questions Peter has brought to me: How do I know that it is truly Astaroth that brings the disease to Peter? How can I be sure that God doesn't want this disease to be with Peter?

Peter is still talking, giving directions. He is pointing at a map on the wall near the door. He finishes with " . . . nestled before that set of mountains, and there you are." He is silent for a moment. "It takes many days, but a healthy person could walk there. Even you. Even a child, if he were healthy." His voice has a touch of heaviness again.

I must keep his mind moving. I ask aimlessly, "Have you read about demons?"

"Much," says Peter.

I take interest. "What do you know about them?"

"Too much to put in a thimble." Peter coughs and leans back into his stacked pillows. He puts his hands together like a philosopher. I can tell he likes the idea of having a grown-up conversation. He fancies himself an authority. He lifts his chin. "Be specific, Ugly Sorceress. Ask precisely what you want to know."

"Be careful," I say. "Do not speak the name of a demon."

Peter nods. "I will be careful."

"Tell me, Peter, when do you feel the worst?"

Peter smiles sadly. "On a morning like today. It is the hot, sunny days, when the other children run and climb and swim and have the most fun, that I am the worst off. In winter sometimes I pass whole days painlessly."

"The darkest days?"

"Yes."

"The dampest days?"

"Yes," says Peter. His voice shows cautious interest. He coughs the wet, deep cough I expected.

I sniff. "And the smell of your bedclothes?"

"It's not my bedclothes," says Peter. "It's me. I'm rotting."

"No," I say. "It's him."

Peter looks at me with the first glimmer of hope in his eyes. "You know who he is?"

"I know," and before the word passes to silence, the air itself takes on weight. It presses on my chest and head. It crushes. My throat constricts. I fight to fill my lungs.

Peter gags. The weight is too much for his weakened frame. He clutches both hands to his throat. I am strong enough for this battle—he is not.

I take the hollow reed from the bowl of broth, grab the sword from the floor, and rush to the head of the bed. I pry the boy's hands from his neck. His eyes meet mine, and suddenly, as though in tacit agreement, he puts his hands behind his head and arches his back. For a brief moment I realize he believes he is surrendering himself. I pray he is wrong. I pierce his throat with the tip of the sword. The blood gushes forth. I know that if this fails, if the boy dies, I will be hanged for murder. I jam the reed into the bloody opening of his throat and blow on one end. His chest rises and falls. I blow again. His chest rises and falls. Rises and falls. Finally the air passes through the reed on its own. I need not blow now.

Peter slowly eases his back down into the bedclothes.

"It is important, Peter, that I summon the devil properly." I am panting. "His name must be pronounced exactly right." And I must hurry, I think. I must hurry before the rigid reed collapses under the heavy air.

Peter touches his lips. I realize he wants to speak. I blow extra air into the reed; then I cover the end so that when he exhales the air will not exit from the reed, but pass instead through his voice box and out his mouth.

His eyes are glued to mine. He trusts me. "Demons do things . . . ," he whispers.

I blow again into the reed and again I cover the end.

" . . . in reverse," he says.

"You're right," I cry. Oh, how could I have been so

foolish? I have not practiced Astaroth's name in reverse in my head. But if I don't call properly, he will not come. What a miserable woman I am! How could I expect to take on the devils when I have never studied the devils? I know less than this bedridden child. Now there is no hope.

As if the devils can read my thoughts, the air is at once weightless again. Astaroth is no longer alarmed. He tastes success. I know he laughs at me. He wants the burgermeister to enter the room now and see his son swathed in blood. He wants the burgermeister to breathe the light air. He steals all support from my excuse. I look at the red-dipped sword helplessly.

I should drop this sham and run.

But, oh, then the boy would die. His skin speaks of imminent death. The hole in his throat provides Astaroth another entry. I must help Peter. He has entered my heart. And he trusts me now. His hope is alive. It doesn't matter what I know or do not know of devils. The boy has saved me from the error of mispronouncing Astaroth's name. God wants me here; otherwise, he never would have put the plaice fish in Asa's hands. Otherwise, he never would have given Peter the interest in demons that allowed him to save us both this time. God is with me. I know this.

I look out the window. The sun is high. It is afternoon.

The shadows will come soon. I cannot run and hide and practice the devil's name in reverse inside my head. And if I try to come another day, the burgermeister will turn me away. He will never allow me to come near Peter again after I have used his own sword on his son. He will lose faith in me. And woe be to the sorceress who loses the faith of the people, for it is among the gravest of crimes to put yourself forth as a sorcerer and not succeed. You will be condemned as not truly a servant of God.

I am dressed in my brown cloak, and I dare not strip down to my white shift in front of this boy. He is young, but not that young. It wouldn't seem right. But even though I'm not dressed in the traditional white of the sorceress, my cloak is good, I know. It has no buttons, buckles, hooks. It has no knots. There is nothing in my cloak that would stop the flow of power from my body.

I pick up the sword. I marvel to see my hand does not shake. Peter keeps his eyes on me. His respiration is loud and labored. I draw a magic circle around the bed. As it nears completion, the reed in Peter's throat suddenly squashes shut. I complete the circle as fast as I can. I sit on the bed with Peter, holding both his hands in mine. His chest is still now. He doesn't breathe. The flow of blood on his throat has slowed to a sluggish welling of drops. His eyes are hot, but he fights the panic. "Htoratsa," I whisper. The word is flawless. Hallelujah. "Leave this child's body. Be gone!"

A hiss of steam rushes around the reed, making it flap piteously. Peter writhes. I pull the reed from his throat and press my thumb over the gaping hole. "Cough, Peter. Cough." I put my face to his and command, "Cough!"

Peter's knees jerk upward and press against his belly. He curls around his middle. It is all I can do to keep my thumb over the hole in his throat. Peter's mouth stretches open wide—wider than I have ever seen a person's mouth open. It is as though his jaw is hinged, like a snake's.

"Cough!" I shout.

He rocks and twists and finally spasms. A yellow river of phlegm shoots out and hits the floor. A foul odor fills the room. Peter coughs again and again, each time adding to the pool of phlegm. His chest is like a barrel that must empty.

Finally, the coughing stops. Slowly, slowly Peter uncurls. He lies back on his pillows. The hole in his throat is closed, though a purple scar has formed. A scar the color of amethyst. He breathes normally.

One look at Peter's eyes tells me Astaroth is gone. "God be with you," I call, to make sure he doesn't return.

Peter looks at me in exhaustion. Then the resilience of

youth manifests itself. He rises from the bed. He stands unsure, as though the floor might shift under him. He puts both hands to his face and smells. "The rot has stopped." He runs one hand up his arm. "My skin is cool again." The whites of his eyes, yellow moments ago, are now the color of thick cream. I know they will be white as clouds before long. He looks at me with wonder. He laughs. He hugs me. "Oh, beautiful sorceress." Then he runs outdoors, shouting to his father.

I am stunned at the word. No one has ever used the word *beautiful* for me before. No one ever will again. It is not the word for a hunchback. I bask in the word for a moment. Then I go outdoors to join the others.

There is much rejoicing all day.

At dusk I am sent home with Asa and Bala. Asa's teeth are smeared with chocolate. She licks it away slowly, lingeringly. She pulls from her pocket a new candy circle of mint and sings a song about it all the way home. She puts it over the doorway, beside the other. Bala has a miniature star sapphire. I have an amethyst from the burgermeister's sword. I will use it to draw magic circles in the future. After all, the plaice head has begun to deteriorate.

Asa and Bala go to bed happy.

I lie awake and think of Peter. Two things trouble me

from today. The easier one is most perilous to my body. I think of how it was Peter's chance words that made me call Astaroth in reverse. Had I said his name normally, the demon would not have come. I could never have driven him off. Peter would have died. And I would have been slain for falsely portraying myself as a sorceress.

I must learn as much as I can about sorcery. I must visit Peter and read his books. I cannot let ignorance endanger my life. God tells me now to do these things. God will not tolerate my bumbling in the future.

But the more troubling thing was Peter's question: "How can you tell what is the work of God and what is the work of the devils?" I must be able to discern the difference or I may run afoul of God. Who am I to think I have the wisdom to tell the difference?

I pass a second night tossing and turning.

In the morning Asa brings me a bucket of crabs. "I used the fish head for bait," she says. "Look how many."

We roast the crabs and eat them. Asa laughs. Her laugh is as clear as a gold bell.

And now I know the answer. Much knowledge can be gained from reading Peter's books, but not this kind of knowledge. No. It isn't up to me to recognize the demons of this world. That is not a human task. God will tell me. All I have to do is listen.

four

BAAL

I sit on the dry grass and look at our cabin. There are circles of green mint stretching from the top of the door up to the pointed roof and down along the eaves all across the front—payment from the many nobles whose families I have served. From here I cannot see the sides of our cabin, but I know the garland of mints goes along the eaves all the way to the back of the house. Perhaps one more year of healing would have brought enough mints to make them meet at the back of the cabin. But the garland will never be complete now.

Asa has lost interest in mints. She is a young woman now. Fourteen years old. She no longer begs Peter to tell her tales of the land of enchanted forests. Asa has other concerns. She dresses in velvet. Her fingers are still bare, for she awaits the perfect ring. But her hair is capped with a lace bonnet. There are ribbons of many colors woven into the strands, and she wears diamonds on the soles of her shoes. No one else knows; no one can see them. No one tries to rob her.

I wear my brown cloak. I know that external beauty is not my fate, despite Peter's remark when first I healed him. The boy was blinded by the joy of health. He has never since called me beautiful, though we see each other weekly. That is as it should be. It is only the eyes of God that see me as beautiful now. And the eyes of God are the only eyes I care about.

But there are other ways that the world sees my value. I am the healer for this region of the world. People travel days, at great personal expense and hardship, to visit me. They are always rewarded for their pains. I am an agent of God.

We live in our cabin still. Asa lives here more to humor me than anything else. She cannot sense the rightness of this cabin as a home, no matter how often I try to explain it to her. I see her walk on the town streets and look with interest at the nobles' homes. I know already that she will marry a noble. Perhaps the son of Geiss the Fat. He has walked toward Asa twice now. Each time I have managed to whisk her away. Geiss the Fat is a puritanical fanatic who would deny his daughter-in-law all beautiful things; I know that. Asa would suffer in his home. Still, soon I will have to give her up. It is right. She is a woman.

I have trouble imagining the cabin without Asa. She would gladly take me with her to any noble's house. That I see in my head, although I have not tried to develop my powers as a seer. But this cabin is where I must stay. It is a humble abode. I cherish the safety of humility.

In the corner of the cabin, in a box made of porcupine quills, is a treasure: more jewels than any noble hereabouts owns. I have told Asa to stay away from the porcupine box and never talk of it to others. No one else dares to enter our cabin—the home of a sorceress. So the jewels are safe. When Asa marries, I will give her the box of jewels as a dowry. She will leave, not by the mercy of a noble, but with his great gratitude for catching her. And I will stay here.

I am like a treasure myself. When I think like this, sometimes a finger of fear makes a cross on my heart. The Patient Scholar who taught me to read alerted me to many perils: Knowing my own value is dangerously close to hubris. I have discussed this with Peter. He has proven himself wise in many matters. He says hubris is a form of vanity, as is all pride. I must not anger God with pride. Yet denying my value would be a lie. It is right to recognize value, and then to know its true source: I am a treasure not because of my intrinsic worth, but because I am an agent of God. I am one of God's jewels. I abide by the lesson of the amethyst.

"Ugly One," hisses Bala.

I know without turning it is Bala. She is the only one left who does not call me Ugly Sorceress. She has come silently across the grasses. Yet even the field mice make this dry grass crackle. I wonder if she has flown. I see a vision: In the next life she is a starling. For an instant I see through her future eyes and I am chilled with my fear of heights. I shudder. But that is not the only reason for my shudder. My vision is impure. Bala could never become a bird—animals have no souls. I do her a disservice to think this way. I banish the vision.

"Peter sends this," says Bala.

I turn and receive the book. Peter has been my source of reading for nine years now. I look at the plain black cover of the book that Peter told me he would send. I open it and stare at the graceful script. It is Hebrew. I know no Hebrew. I will sit in the sun and let God translate this ancient testament for me. Peter thinks there is something important in the text. He is sure there are passages about vanity that will touch me. I did not ask Peter where the passages were. I start at the beginning.

"How did you learn to read?" asks Bala suddenly.

I feel uncomfortable under the scrutiny of her eye. She suspects me of something. But there is no evil in knowing how to read. So her suspicion is really just jealousy. "A scholar taught me," I say as disarmingly as I can. I fight the color that wants to come to my cheeks at the mention of my Patient Scholar.

"Why would a scholar bother with you?"

"My mother asked him," I say unwillingly, which is partly true. My Patient Scholar began teaching me for my mother's sake. But he continued teaching me for the sake of a different bond—a bond that strengthened each time I saw him.

A flash of memory crosses Bala's eyes. "Your mother did many unusual things."

I hold the book tightly. "I am an ordinary peasant, like you, Bala. The only difference is that I read. If you like, I will teach you."

She laughs. "The only differences are that you read *and* that you are a sorceress."

I hope her laugh is sincere.

"The Baron von Oynhausen's newborn has an extra

finger," says Bala quickly. "They are bringing her to you this afternoon."

I pay little attention. An extra finger is a trifle. This search for physical perfection is uninteresting to me. It is pain and disease that I want to eradicate. But I will shrivel the finger.

I know without calling forth all demons that it is Baal's work. Baal has three heads, and out of spite, he causes extra fingers, toes, even eyes to form on newborns. I look at the sky. "Bala, run tell the baron that he must come before noon." I know that Baal never cooperates after noon. "Run."

"The baron won't like that," says Bala. "He has traveled for four days to come to you. He wants to rest before the ordeal." Bala shakes her head. "Don't antagonize him."

I think of Bala's name and Baal's name. A simple permutation of letters turns one into the other. I never noticed before. I look her up and down, but I see no evidence of extra parts. "Tell him," I say.

Bala leaves, muttering. I cannot hear her words.

I open the yellowed pages of Peter's tome. The language is sparse and poetic. It sings to me. I read for hours.

The morning passes, and the baron arrives late in the

afternoon. He is pompous and blustering. If I send him away, there is little chance that he will take it gracefully. If I call up Baal, there is no chance that he will cooperate.

But the finger is an easy problem. I hold the tiny hand in mine. The extra finger goes out to one side. I can solve this problem without summoning Baal. I can easily bite off the finger. A simple midwife's job, and I am, beneath it all, a simple midwife.

No one must see me bite the finger. I take the baby in my arms.

"Where are you going?" The baron blocks my path.

"The baby and I must be alone," I say, my eyes on the floor in the position of humility that the baron requires.

"Where is your magic amethyst that I have heard much of? The one of a violet so sharp it stuns." His voice betrays more than the worry of a father whose baby has an extra finger. He wants to do this thing, whatever this thing may be, right—and he has no idea where to begin. He needs something solid to place his faith in.

I pull the amethyst from my cloak and hold it up for his inspection. I do not tell him that the brilliance of its hue is merely evidence of the iron impurities within. He would be flustered. He may be a dullard of sorts. I sympathize. I want to soothe him. I hold the amethyst closer to his face.

"Draw your magic circle here. I will watch."

"It is dangerous, Sire," I say, my eyes on the ground. "The baby and I will be within the magic circle. We will be protected. But those outside the circle are vulnerable."

The baron clears his throat. "I will watch." He leans over my stooped body and lowers his voice so no one else can hear. "How far away must I stand to be safe?"

I make the simple calculation in my head. If he stands by the pond and I am in the birch grove, he can see our forms and be reassured the baby is there. But he will not be able to see my mouth close around the finger. "Come," I say.

I plant him by the pond and carry the baby up into the grove. The baby sleeps in my arms.

I pull out the amethyst and hold it up to catch the sun. I want the baron to see. I draw a magic circle, knowing that I will not use it. The baron knows nothing.

I set the amethyst on the ground inside the circle. I need it not.

The baby nuzzles against my breast. I lean over her and bite away the finger with one swift gnash of the teeth. The baby shrieks. I put my finger to the open wound and sing. My voice is raspy and old, but my words are charmed. The infant's sobs are hiccoughs now.

My ears catch the noise. Life stirs in the dry brush. I

look. A field mouse has strayed into the open. It nudges at something yellow in the dirt just outside the line of the magic circle.

I watch as the baby's hiccoughs subside and she sleeps again. The yellow is light and dark. Gold. The mouse gives a flick of the nose, and the ring flops over. I can see all of it now. It reminds me of something. Grape leaves with clusters of grapes. Spanish gold. I think back to Otto of the West Forest. Is this the ring his wife wore? The ring I marveled at so many years ago, before I ever thought of joining the league of healers? And, yes, there is the figure eight in the middle. But the ring is on its side, and now I see. Oh, yes. I laugh at my own stupidity. It is not an eight at all. It is the snake that swallows its own tail—it is the infinity symbol.

The ring's glory shines warmly. It seems almost liquid, like the purest gold. And now it comes to me as a revelation: The ring's essence is holy. The precious stones that nobles have given me—Asian rubies and sapphires, African diamonds—all shine with earthly beauty. Even the amethyst I use to draw the magic circle was not holy on its own—it became holy through being blessed. But this gold shines with heavenly beauty. With an intrinsic holiness. I want that holiness. I want the lordly gold. I want the purest mineral of all to mark my purest of souls. I want all to see this ring adorn my heavenly beauty.

The mouse scurries off. The baby sniffles in its sleep. The blood has already stopped flowing. The world is at peace, waiting for me to act. I look again at the ring.

The ring is perfect. And, oh, yes, of course, the ring is not for me. How could I make such a mistake? Asa awaits the perfect ring. Have I not thought this just today? This ring is for Asa. Of course. The ring will adorn her, and, in turn, her glow will light my world. Oh, yes.

Yet the ring lies outside the magic circle. Would that I could call the mouse back to flip the ring within the circle. But what am I thinking? I have summoned no demons. There is no reason to suspect that demons lie outside the circle. And since I am pure of heart, no demon that is not summoned can harm me even outside the circle. I am giddy with anticipation. I laugh. I laugh with the inebriation of the rapture to come. When I am in control of myself once more, I plan my actions. I will slip on the ring and hide my hand in the folds of my cloak. Later, when I am home alone with Asa, I will present it to her. I can see her loving face. Oh, what grace God has given us.

I reach my fingers tentatively toward the ring.

It glows.

I am touching the magic circle's periphery now.

The ring dazzles.

I slide my index finger into the ring.

I am snatched from the circle. The baby falls to the ground and wails. I am squeezed until I feel the breath of life going. I cannot shout.

Voices hiss around my ears. "We have you. At last."

"You were not summoned," I want to say. But I have no breath.

As if Baal can read my thoughts, his three voices say, "When you bit the finger, you released us."

But I bit off fingers when I was a midwife, I am thinking, and you never came then.

"It is you who drew the magic circle, you who made this moment a challenge. We merely rose to the challenge. We are permitted to accept a challenge." The voices laugh in a three-part harmony. "Heavenly beauty! Look at your heavenly beauty! See how they gape at your heavenly beauty!" The voices are raucous. "Throw away your amethyst. You will no longer summon devils. Instead, we will summon you!" The laughter is like the screaming of wildcats. "You are no longer the Ugly Sorceress. You are the Ugly Witch."

The light is fading. I feel darkness about to overtake me. I want my ears to go deaf. I must not allow myself to hear the words I know will come. I have been pronounced a witch. There is an order to come—oh, damned and hellish order. I must not hear it. I hold my palms tight over my ears.

But the voices are too clever for me. They bypass my ears entirely. They speak inside my head. "Eat the child."

I close my mind. Demons are stupid, not clever. I must not think they are clever. They are stupid. All of them, every last one, was tricked into devilhood by the acts of Satan. If Satan could trick them, so can I.

"Stupid, are we?" The voices boom inside my head. "No one tricks us. Eat that baby!"

I am thrown on the ground. My ribs split. The air rushes back into my lungs. I breathe unwillingly. "Never," I say.

The laughter is deafening. "You have but one choice."

"I will never serve the forces of evil," I scream.

And suddenly footsteps are loud and multiple. The baron's men rush at me from every direction. They come out from behind every tree.

"She's a witch!"

"I saw her eat the finger!"

"She works with devils!"

"Burn her!"

The air is filled with starlings.

five

Fire

"What proof do you have?" Peter's voice rises over the rest.

I cannot look at him as they stack the wood at Asa's and my feet. Only forty-eight hours have passed since I was arrested in the birch grove, yet it seems an eternity. Asa has said nothing up to this point. Her face is slack. Her mouth hangs partway open. Her eyes are glassy. We are tied to a young birch tree. They are saying the birch is now evil, because the grove has been my healing place.

I cannot look at Peter—if he sees my eyes, he will know it is true; I am a witch. I cannot bear to see the pain that would bring him.

"Show me proof, or she goes free." Peter's voice is loud and deep.

"The witch-marks," screams Tzipi, Tzipi whose children I brought into this world. Tzipi, whom no other midwife would help because she is not Christian. Tzipi, who gave me the very first ribbon for Asa's hair. If anyone should be loyal to me in this moment, it is Tzipi. But, of course, if anyone cannot afford to be loyal to me, it is Tzipi. For the others would spring upon her at the slightest provocation. Tzipi has always been in danger. She can only strengthen herself by denouncing me now. Oh, wretched Tzipi.

If I could cry, I would. I would wail, for Tzipi and Asa and Peter and myself. But witches have no tears.

My eyes turn to Tzipi, and I can see her old age ahead. I know her son Erik will die before his wife gives birth. I know that within Tzipi a cancer will languidly lick its way from organ to organ. I could have stopped it. I could have healed her, but for this ring that will not budge from my index finger no matter how hard I rip at it.

I hate the ring now. It was for desire of the ring that I lost all grace. I want to throw the ring away, though it would be a futile gesture. The ring is not the source of evil—it has no power. I know my own image of myself as heavenly destroyed me. Vain image. I forgot the lesson of the amethyst. Oh, wretched drunken stupor that goes by the name of hubris!

Still, I would be rid of this ring before I die if only I could. I would bite my finger off, if my hands were not tied behind my back. My teeth are iron now. I could bite my own leg in two. And no blood would I taste. I have no blood. Everything about me is witchery.

"Show me!" Peter kicks his way through the woodpile. "Show me!" he shouts. He is a strong young man now. I am proud of his strength. And I burn with that pride. It is my pride, no one else's. I can no longer even think the name of the one whose hands I used to roll in. I am alone. There is no reason to fight pride any longer. I am excruciatingly alone.

Tzipi rips my cloak open. On my right arm, where there never was a mole before, there is now a large black one.

"A common mole!" Peter touches the mole. "See." He holds his finger up. "I am not harmed. It is a common mole."

Suddenly the one black mole breaks into a cluster of moles that forms an eight-pointed star. Tzipi shrieks. She steps backward, hands to her cheeks, shaking her head from side to side. "The mark of the incubi."

It is not the mark of incubi; I know that. Incubi are

male demons that mate with sleeping women. No demon has mated with me. I have not slept since I became a witch, two afternoons ago in this birch grove. I will never sleep again.

Peter stares at the mole star. His head is bent over my arm. I feel his tears fall on my skin. They turn to ice as they touch me. "No," he sobs, quickly brushing the ice pearls away before anyone else can see.

"Stand aside." A small man in red robes stands in front of me. "I am Herr Pastor Dean Hartmann von Rosenbach of the Wurzburg Cathedral. I have traveled great distances at the request of the Baron von Oynhausen. You must listen to me, for I am the mouth of God." He holds a pin the length of his hand. He turns to the crowd. "Another proof?" He points at Peter. "Is that what this misguided young man needs?" He brandishes the pin like a sword. Swiftly he lifts my cloak and runs his fingers across my thighs. He stops at the scar I got as a child, falling from a beech tree. The fall that left me terrified of heights. He jabs the pin fiercely into the scar. The pain is like lightning radiating from the metal. He pulls the pin out just as suddenly. My flesh closes over the hole. No blood appears. The pastor lets my cloak drop. He opens his hands toward the crowd. "Unquestionable, undeniable truth. The Ugly One, this ill-intended midwife, who says she heals and thus thwarts the efforts of our real and verified surgeons, this one . . ." He points to me with his chin, then turns back to the crowd and shouts, "This one is a witch!"

"But she's in shock," shouts Peter. "People in shock don't bleed."

The pastor has turned heel and is climbing over the woodpile to the crowd.

"And you stabbed her in the thigh, in the fattest part of the body." Peter's voice rises in a screech. "Blood runs the thinnest there." He is hysterical now. "And it was on a scar. Scar tissue doesn't bleed."

The pastor is lost in the crowd.

I look at Peter and rage with pride at his knowledge of anatomy—the knowledge I imparted to him in our weekly discussions. The irony of the situation does not escape me. I fight the laughter that would burst from my throat.

And now the crowd has pushed Peter back. The woodpile is growing, as though it is a thing alive. I hear a flutter and look toward it. Bala stands in the crowd. Her eyes meet mine. I cannot read behind her eyes, though I try. Is she the incarnation of the demon Baal? I have been asking myself this for the past forty-eight hours. I have looked for clues in Bala's words and actions of the past nine years. I can find no clear evidence. But even if she is Baal, what does that mean? Can she help who she is? Was she trapped like me? Did she long for a bauble, or was her weakness more worthy of sympathy than mine? Is all evil the result of entrapment? I want to talk with Bala, if only for a moment. I have been kept in isolation since I bit the child's finger off. I have talked with no one, not even Asa. But I must talk with Bala; I must know her secret, if she harbors one. My mind reaches out to hers. I fail; her mind is shut to me, her eyes filmed over. The crowd presses on her, and she retreats.

The ache in my thigh is unrelenting.

Peter scrabbles once more across the woodpile. But this time he grabs Asa's arm. He pulls up the velvet sleeves. On both arms there is a ring of green moles, like a circle of green mint. The devils are making a game of our demise. They think they are clever. Peter wipes a tear from his cheek and wets Asa's arm with it. It does not turn to ice. "Asa is not a witch!" Peter lifts both arms above his head and shouts so that the veins in his neck stand out like ropes. "Asa is not a witch!"

A large man pulls Peter away with one hand and pours pitch on the wood with the other. He is Wilhelm Lutz, I am sure. I delivered him. He resembles his mother. A pious woman. These are all pious people. Pious witch burners.

"Cry, Asa," shouts Peter. "Show them you are not a witch."

Asa's eyes register briefly on Peter. "Cry?"

The big Wilhelm lights the fire. As the glow rises, a hush falls across the crowd. The only noise is the deafening crack of the fire.

I focus on the women's faces. Many of them are looking around nervously. As the flames grow, the fear in their eyes begins to subside. They realize they have been lucky this time—they have not been denounced as witches. All women are in danger of the frivolous denunciation. Oh, would that my own denunciation had been frivolous! I would give anything to burn here as a holy woman, falsely accused, rather than as the witch I know I am.

But then the voices start within my head. "Work for us."

I have no hesitation. "No."

"Work for us, and we will give you the gift of metamorphosis. You can turn into the salamander of vermillion. You will be fireproof. You can slink away into the woodpile, and they'll never find you."

"No," I say.

"The work is easy. Easier than sorcery."

"Never," I say.

And now the voices are silent. And only one thought repeats itself quietly in the back of my mind. "Work for us, and we will save Asa."

Trade my soul so that my daughter can stay on this earth, in this brief interlude we call life. What kind of trade is that?

"She's going to burn if you don't agree. Her blood will boil. Her eyes will burst. Her skin will split. And still she will be alive and feel every cell's agony. We will keep her alive to the very last moment."

"No," I force myself to say.

"And she will blame you. She is blaming you already for the pain. She is cursing you."

My Asa is cursing me.

"She hates you."

Asa's first scream pierces my soul. Her skirt is on fire.

"Yes," I say to the devils, as though my tongue has a life of its own. "Yes, I will do your work. Save Asa."

"Cry!" screams Peter, over the roar of the fire. "Cry, Asa. Don't scream, cry!"

And Asa is crying, tears streaming down her face. The ropes that bind her hands are suddenly loose and she holds her arms out for all to see. The moles are gone.

Peter leaps into the fire and drags Asa to safety. They

are rolling in the brush. They are screaming with pain. They are wet with tears. I think I hear "Mother." I want to hear it.

"Asa is not a witch," says Bala loudly. "It is only the Ugly One."

"Asa is not a witch," says another voice.

"Asa is not a witch."

A group carries Asa and Peter away to the stream. Asa is struggling. Is she trying to get free of them, to come to me? Or is she writhing in pain from her burns?

I am left with my cloak afire. The heat within me brings exquisite pain. My skin peels into chips not unlike the bark of a black cherry. And in a second the pain ceases. My cloak collapses into the flames. I slink out of the gold ring that encircled my finger before and now encircles my smooth belly. It melts in a sudden puddle that bubbles and boils. I crawl quickly into the woodpile, knowing how to be a salamander against my will. I learn the folk wisdom is wrong: Salamanders are not so cold they can put out fires. The fire rages on. But I am so cold it does not scald me. I shiver. Why does so much of life just happen to us? I would have gladly perished. But it was the trade. I was not allowed to perish. Asa is alive. It is a malignant trade. An evil trade. But I have made it, and nothing can reverse it. I am polluted. I am wicked.

"She's gone! She disappeared!"

"She burned up. There was nothing to her. No blood, no guts. The witch is a burst bubble."

I am in the smoking earth now, digging along. And now in the grasses. It is a long way to the cabin. I could make it in another form much faster. But a salamander will not be seen. I crawl diligently all night. By dawn I arrive. The cabin is closed. I sense the villagers in their homes. They are waiting for full sunlight before they loot. They are afraid that spirits lurk in the shadows of the cabin. I haven't much time. I resume my old form—the form of the Ugly One. I tie the porcupine-quill box to my chest. It is small but heavy. I peer out into the dim light. No one is about yet. I long to walk forth as me, even naked as I am now. But among these villagers I can never be me again. I become a weasel. A common, quick weasel. I must move swiftly and quietly. I must be surreptitious.

A group of women gathers by the stream. Bala is in their midst. They are preparing to loot; I know that. I want to hide the box somewhere that Asa can find it. I stay at a distance and listen hard. Just one word of Asa, that's all I want. And suddenly I realize that Asa cannot have the jewels in this treasure box. They would take them from her for sure. The jewels serve no one now.

And what about my Asa? Will she be taken care of? An orphan without a dowry. But I know Peter will see her through. Maybe Peter will even marry her. I want to know that future, but I cannot. There are walls in my knowledge. If I climb those walls, I must be ready to know whatever lies on the other side. I am not ready. There is some knowledge I must never let myself know.

I run at first randomly. Just away. Keeping far from villages. But then I find I am on a southern path. When I come to a lake, I know I must metamorphose once more. But not to a fish other fish might eat. Nor to one that villagers might try to catch. I must be as revolting to others as I am to myself. I know what I must become. I change—now primitive and efficient. I am eyeless. My mouth puckers. My head is adorned with fleshy horns. I ooze into the water, full of hate for myself. I am a slime eel. I hold the treasure box dry on my tongue. I travel from lake to lake. The lakes are many and large. But the water is cool and fresh. Fresh water, like what runs in my veins now. No more salty tears for me. No more tears of any sort. Witches are doomed to be dry-eyed forever. Oh, blessed tears of the pure of heart! What I would give for the privilege of tears again.

I travel endlessly. Now I learn to curse my fear of heights—for flying would be so much faster. On land I am ever the untrustworthy weasel. In the waters of the great river I have reached at last I am ever the despised slime eel. I keep my ears open for sounds that betray humans. If I cross the path of a human family, I may not be strong enough to resist the voices inside my head. They will demand I eat a human child. This is the initiation rite; this is what separates a witch from all her past for the rest of eternity. But the animals I pass are no threat to me, nor I to them. They have no souls. The devils do not waste their energies with animals. They do not urge me to eat them.

I travel night and day, always against the current, always fleeing. When a voice begins in my head, I shout, "Away. I am going away," until the voice weakens to nothing. I am dredging my mind for my first conversation with Peter. He told me about the book under his pillows. He told me about a special land where wolves eat grandmothers and young beggar girls are princesses for a night. He told me that land is full of enchanted forests. That is the land whose stories Peter recited so often to my Asa. That is the land she loved.

The book under Peter's pillows is more real to me now than any so-called sacred book. The land in that book is more alluring than heaven. I think of the first book my Patient Scholar introduced me to. I remember the joy that permeated my spirit. The joy that settled in my heart through the years as I read each book. I realize now that I never got to the passage on vanity in Peter's tome that he so much wanted me to read. Would that passage have saved me? Would it have kept me from lusting for the ring? But there is no purpose in thinking of Peter's tome now. It is back in my cabin. Or was. It may now be ashes.

I must think of Peter's other book. The book that stirred his child soul—that made him want to ride on a deer's back—that made my Asa's eyes shine with wonder. I will go to the special land of the book. I will go into a forest, an enchanted forest where no human being will dare to tread. If I am not in the presence of humans, I can do them no harm. What will it matter if I am a witch, if I never work the evil of the demons? I will live in isolation. Safe isolation. Oh, even merry isolation.

The directions Peter gave as I was thinking of other things that first day I met him, the directions my conscious mind never heard, those most important directions are all stored perfectly in my deepest mind. I follow them now. I follow them tirelessly.

I see at last the mountains and I know that the enchanted forest nestles in the foothills.

six

CANDY

I am boiling beets. The beets grow wild, but in more profusion than would have occurred if I hadn't nurtured them along. My beet field covers a wide swath that runs in a half-moon shape to the south of my home. The smell from my pot is sweet, as only beets close to pollination time can be. The water that came from the clear mountain brook nearby is now thick and soupy. I am making beet syrup for my candy.

Above my door, up to the roof peak, along the eaves, and yes, in truth entirely around the house, runs a garland of pink peppermint candies. The peppermint is a green plant, but the round candies are pink from the beet syrup. In all these years I have found no way to take the red color from the beet. So all the candy that covers my house is red to rose to pink. I would love to have it be green, like the mints Asa put on our cabin so long ago. Still, it may be better that it is not green, for green would have made the memory of Asa so strong I might not be able to bear it. And the beet color is pleasing. Luscious rose brittles capture the light in air bubbles that seem to move on a sunny day. They line the outer walls. Bright red buttery caramels form a cornice on every window. Palest of jellied gumdrops stick up in cone-shaped mounds along the roof. I know they are all delicious, though I do not indulge myself. Their sight is enough of a pleasure. The entire log house is decorated with candies. I've achieved a harmony of lights and darks that would bring a flush to my Asa's face. I know that. Or maybe I just fool myself into believing that.

I have changed. I do not indulge myself in memories of Asa. When I first came to these enchanted woods, I thought of her. And her image would come to me so strongly, her smell, her feel, that it was all I could do to keep from racing back, through lakes and forests, to hold her again. I no longer think of her, for if I do, the knowledge of her life will come to me, and I will not be able to resist any longer. And so I no longer know what Asa would like or dislike. I only imagine. I only dream.

I have changed in other ways, too. Never have I yielded to the temptation to use magic, though in my hours in bed I am told formulas for bleaching the beet syrup. When I arise—not awaken, no, just arise, for I never sleep; I will never open my body to the incubi that used to hang in my corners like cobwebs waiting for sleep to overtake me—when I arise, I wipe the formulas from my mind and go to work boiling beets. Or, if it is not near the pollination season, I busy myself with other tasks.

There is so much to be done when one lives outside society. I collect wood for the fire every day. I tend a garden for food, and now and then I catch a brook trout. But when I eat a fish, I smoke it whole, so that red blood never falls before my eyes. I cannot risk the temptation of blood, not even that of the animals. The house is in constant need of repair, to stand against the ravages of weather and time. I repair logs and replace those too damaged for repair. I take care to keep every corner slightly askew, for I know that ninety-degree angles invite demons. I am proud of this house, in my paganistic way. I cannot thank the one of huge hands for this house. I built it all alone, with no blessing and no magic. It was difficult. I was not young and I was not large and I was not strong.

The form I live in is my own. I am a hunchbacked old

woman. But I have iron teeth, and ice water runs in my veins. These teeth, though, these formidable weapons, they have never smashed a bone yet. Of this also I am proud, with a raging pride that burns the insides of my eyeballs.

I must relax. The rage of pride is not the only rage that violates me. Another rage is real and demands respect. It is a justified rage. I have lost everything I loved, all by trickery. I have lost the right to roll in the hands I served so well. Ahhh, there it is. I say I served those hands well. I am poisoned with pride still. Oh, most hideous and hateful demons, if you are listening now, listen closely. I will beat you yet. I will never never never practice your evil. You have won nothing. I have outwitted you thus far. I will outwit you forever.

I listen. They do not respond. They never respond these days. Their silence mocks me, and that mocking nourishes my hate.

The rage burns brighter inside me, and I must relax. I am conscious of breathing this oxygen that rusts our bodies into dust. Part of me wants to breathe faster, ever faster, to speed along my own disintegration. But I know the other danger. I know I must breathe slowly. I must not feed the fire of inner rage with oxygen. For if the rage wins, the devils win.

I listen harder. I hear no devils inside my head. Maybe they are not mocking me. Maybe they are truly absent. I have kept the rage so well hidden for so long that they may have abandoned me. There is nothing in me to give them energy. I am not fuel for them. Yes, I believe they stay away.

My eyes light now on the wooden bowl that sits on the shelf above my bed. It is carved into intricate geometric designs. There is no coloring to spoil the purity of the white wood. This bowl took me years to carve. I have smoothed out the inside with sand. Even now I can sit of an evening and rub the bowl with sand to make the inner surface ever more glasslike. The beauty of the bowl stuns my eye. The bowl is a shrine of sorts. It is a shrine to the memory of my daughter.

Four years ago a vision came to me of Asa giving birth to twins. I would not follow the vision; yet behind my conscious knowledge of the world, I hold this vision sacred. Once, only once, I took out the vision and held it up to the light like I used to hold our jewels. And my mouth watered with hunger. My own mouth—my own grandchildren.

The vision must be sealed away.

The rage must not win.

I have lived here nine years now. The same amount

of time that I served as a sorceress. At first I was never alone. They sent me imps. The earliest imps were wolves. I asked them if they ate grandmothers, and they smiled slyly. I offered them beet skin to gnaw on. They ran off.

Then came the small cats. They rubbed around my ankles and made me yearn for human contact. So I went to the hawthorn and wrapped my ankles in brambles that kept the cats at a distance. They mewed piteously. So I went to the dandelions and stuffed my ears with milkweed. They lay about the floor in piles, licking one another, being a family, breaking the heart I no longer have. So I went to the belladonna plant and chewed and chewed until my pupils opened so wide I could not see. Never did I use magic. The cats ran off.

And, of course, through it all were the nets of beauty, strung out to entrap me. For years I was wary of these nets. I was on the lookout for minerals—the precious stones and metals that had marked my nine years as a sorceress. I expected the spray of the lake in a storm to turn to emeralds. I expected raindrops to turn to diamonds. I planned my response: I would gaze impassively upon the gems, then look away. But the devils knew I'd never touch another crystal. They didn't waste their time. Instead, they sent a different type of ornament.

Once when I was following a natural path barefoot

through these great southern fir trees, the path itself turned to velvet black stones. I picked up a stone and realized it was jet. Against my will, my eyes saw how the jet would shine with a vigorous polish. I wanted to throw it away—to hurl it at the skies. But I knew better. I placed it down gently, exactly where I'd picked it up from, and walked home and put on shoes. I never went barefoot again.

Another day I was raiding a honeycomb when a large chunk of brown tumbled from the rotting tree. When it hit the ground, it split, exposing the golden honey glow of amber. I patiently set the honeycomb back in the tree trunk and turned my back on the amber. I went home. And I trained my tongue to favor rosemary, savory, and thyme. No more sweets for me. No more visits to the honey tree. From that day on I even forbade myself the taste of my own candies.

Yet another day I knelt on the shore of a large lake and let the sand sift through my fingers for the sheer silky pleasure. The grains of sand turned to pearls. They glistened with the white innocence of Asa's soul. I wanted to form a cup with my hands and drink of them. Instead, I brushed off my hands and stripped and swam in the cold waters until I was numb.

Nature's beauty turned ornamental, fashioned from

plants and animals—these things lure me not. Nor do the surprisingly fragrant orchids, which come in shameless profusion. Nor do the yellow clouds of canaries, the melodious birds that were unknown to me before I came to this land. No assault on my vision or smell or hearing can win.

I cannot be tempted by that which lived or lives, any more than I can be tempted by that which never lived.

Eventually these assaults on my senses ended. Or, rather, eventually I stopped noticing them. Or, in truth, eventually, though I still noticed, the callouses on my spirit prevented wounds. I am impervious to nature's perfection.

Sometimes I catch a spider regarding me silently. I move closer. Once a sunbeam split through dew on a web and danced all colors along my eaves. But I turned my eyes to the spider alone. To the spider's eyes. I always look carefully in a spider's eyes. And sometimes I think I see a spark of fury in those eyes. I allow no impish cobwebs in my home. I sweep with a broom made from the witch-hazel bush. Fitting name, I think.

Imps usually come to witches to help them perform their evil magic. Since I perform no magic, their presence cannot be mistaken for a cordiality. And since I am immune to temptation, they are not here to lure me. They have but one purpose: They are spies. The furious spiders that appear on my walls, on my pillow, in my cupboards less and less frequently in these last few years, they are all spies. I rub the shelves with vinegar each day, outlawing the dust that can hide spiders. My home smells of fermentation, but it is a clean acidity. It is the best that I can do. The energy I once focused on healing and loving the divine being now works to keep the devils at bay.

At times, though, I am alone. Totally alone. I believe I am alone now.

I am setting the beet juice outside to cool when the doe runs past, fear making her hooves fleet. I do not ask her why she runs. I could, but I resist. Years ago, when I sat quietly on the south side of a hill admiring a fox family lolling about outside their den in the warm morning sun, the serpent devil slithered up behind me and licked my ears. Instantly I could hear the loving encouragement the vixen gave her kits. I fled, full of the pain of loss. From that moment on, I have understood the language of every animal, large and small. Yet I never talk with them. I know their company would only make the forbidden idea of human company more attractive. I learned that lesson from the vixen. I do not even allow myself to eavesdrop. I must shut my ears now so that I cannot hear this doe's anguish.

A flock of starlings is startled. They rise into the air in a noisy cloud of black and yellow. I hate starlings, of course.

And a family of squirrels is racing by. The younger ones are curious, running back to the source of the fear, disappearing for many minutes, then racing on ahead again.

I am not curious myself. Curiosity is an innocent emotion. I am only anxious. I shut myself in my candy house and build a fire. Most living creatures are afraid of fire. I grab my witch-hazel broom and hold it ready to thrust into the fire. I can use it like a torch if I must defend myself. I wish I could light a starling afire.

Suddenly my window breaks. That window of spun-sugar glass. The pink shards melt in the heat from the burning bird. A starling lies on my floor enveloped in a red and yellow sphere. My ears hurt from its silent shriek. Before my eyes the flaming wings turn to ash and nothing is left but smoke.

Oh, why did I allow myself a wish? Oh, dreadful wish. I fall to my knees and lean over what isn't there any longer. I have exercised an evil power without meaning to. The very fact that the devils have left me alone for so long is a type of seduction. I have been seduced into killing this bird. After nine long years I am still vulnerable. Oh, misery that owns my heart. I must stay on guard always, even if the devils are distant. For the evil power is mine always. It is a task not to use that power. A wearisome, difficult task. I must be vigilant.

I leave the safety of the hearth and walk to my bed. I lie down and shut my eyes. I will not sleep.

And yet I feel the sleep overtaking me. My eyelids are thick and wet as lily pads. I tell myself I could easily open them, but I don't want to right now. It is by choice that I lie here with shut eyes. My choice. Yes.

I don't know if I slept. It is possible, for as the voices come to me, I feel that I am awakening. But the voices are not within my head. My body freezes. The voices are outside my home.

"Throw me down some gumdrops, Hansel," says a light, high voice. The sound is musical, but the words cut me as deeply as any sword. A child is outside my home. A human child!

"Here, Gretel."

I hear the sound of something breaking from my roof.

The child named Gretel laughs. "Maybe we won't starve, after all." Her laughter is not totally gleeful. A hint of panic whets her voice.

I am totally alert. I am scanning my deepest thoughts. I find nothing to be afraid of. Yet I must not let down my guard. I remember how my mouth watered at the vision of my own grandchildren. I am not trustworthy.

"Candy is good, Gretel," says the child Hansel. "All the time they've been lying to us. Candy is wonderful."

"Hush. Don't say wicked thoughts. We are eating this candy only because we need to," says Gretel with a full mouth. "Recall the pastor's words. We must deny pleasures of the flesh. We are not eating this candy by choice. We are not sinners." There is fear in her voice. Her pastor is a powerful force.

"I'm eating it because I like it," says Hansel.

A smacking sound comes from Gretel's mouth. I know her tongue is working at the sticky gumdrop in her teeth. "It is sweet, I admit." She gives a small, childlike laugh. "Very sweet. And the cottage is so beautiful. I cannot believe how beautiful it is. It is like heaven itself."

Her voice is full of awe. These children are agog at my home. The girl Gretel called it a cottage. The word sounds warm and cozy and happy. I feel myself standing up, not knowing what I am going to do next.

"Oh, this one has peppermint flavor. Gretel, taste this." There is the sound of something breaking from my roof again.

I am slightly giddy. I speak, but my voice is musical, not my old, rough peasant's voice. No, it is the gentle voice of a friend. I am saying, "Nibble nibble like a mouse. Who is nibbling at my house?" My words are sweet as the candy the children eat.

"It is only the wind," says Hansel from the roof.

What a foolish, innocent child. Would that all of us could be so innocent.

I open the front door and look upon the little girl in braids. Her eyes open wide at my ugliness. She drops the gumdrop, even though her whole body is aching for its nourishment. Her hands fly up to cover her mouth.

"Don't be afraid," my sweet voice says. "You must be tired, and I can see you are hungry. I'll feed you."

The girl lowers her hands. The boy drops from the roof. He is younger and suffering even more from lack of food. They look at me with fear and hope. The bitter hunger of creeping starvation burns from those eyes.

"I am ugly, it is true," I say. "But you know better than to be afraid of outer appearances."

The girl motions to the boy to come by her side. He obeys. He trusts her. I admire that trust.

"Come inside," I say.

Gretel stands motionless. Hansel looks up at her. Then he looks at me. He wants to come inside.

"I have known the pain of hunger," I say. "And I have

known the pain of loneliness. I can help you. Come inside."

Hansel takes a step forward. Gretel pulls him back.

"You are a wise and careful girl," I say to Gretel.

"Who are you?" she says at last. Her voice is young and open and human. It is everything I am not.

"I am an old woman. I live alone. I have a simple life."

Gretel seems to gather courage from my words. "I am Gretel. This is my brother, Hansel. What is your name?"

"You can call me Old Woman." I step back so she can see the inside of my home. The kitchen table is within view. A bowl of wild cherries I gathered only yesterday sits there invitingly.

The girl licks her lower lip. Her eyes suddenly become decisive. She walks up and takes my hand. She is older than my grandchildren. But the roundness of her cheeks is familiar. If I could love these children, I would. Her eyes are forceful. I recognize that she is trying to win me over. Hunger has made her desperate. But there is no need for her to work so hard at winning me. I have an instinctive attraction for her.

We go into the candy-bedecked house.

seven

COOKING

Endive soup," I am saying, "is good for you."

"With chicken to flavor it," says Gretel. She pulls a chicken wishbone from her pocket. "I saved this from the last time we had chicken. More than a year ago. It was delicious." Her eyes shine with the hope of satisfying the hunger that makes her cheeks twitch. "I brought it with me for good luck." She puts the wishbone carefully back in her pocket. "We need a chicken thigh. A nice, juicy chicken thigh." She licks her top lip. "The dark meat and blood would add flavor."

I look at her sharply, afraid the voices will start in my head. "And how is it one so small as you knows the art of the kitchen?"

"I helped my mother cook," says Gretel. "She called out what I was to do as she spun wool, and I followed the directions."

"I helped, too," says Hansel. "I brought Mother the wool."

"You have a flock of sheep, then?" I ask doubtfully. These children wear old, tired garments. They haven't the look of children whose parents own animals.

"Oh, no," says Hansel. "I gathered bush wool."

I am confused. I look to Gretel for an explanation.

Gretel laughs. "You know, the tufts that remain when flocks are transferred from one grazing area to the next. I showed Hansel how to collect it. That was before our mother died." Gretel rummages through my small collection of pots and pans as she talks. "I enjoy cooking."

"Your mother is dead," I say softly. Orphans have come to me.

"But our father is alive," says Hansel, sitting at the table, swinging his short, stubby legs.

"And he has married a most wretched woman," says Gretel.

"A real witch," says Hansel.

His words hurt my ears.

"She sent us into the woods, thinking we would die right away." Gretel has chosen a pot. She rubs out the inside with her filthy skirt and smells it. I would smile at her vain effort if I were not afraid of offending this earnest child. The pot obviously has passed her test, for she now sets it on the kitchen table. "We wouldn't have even gotten lost except for the fact that Hansel is so stupid."

"I'm not stupid," says Hansel.

"Putting bread crumbs in your pockets instead of stones was very stupid, Hansel. Your brain is pea-sized." Gretel speaks with great audacity, I am thinking, for one who came so close to starvation's door.

"What is this story of bread crumbs and stones?" I ask.

"Well, the first time our stepmother sent us out in the woods—"

"Our wicked stepmother," says Hansel.

"Yes, our wicked stepmother," says Gretel. "The first time, I told Hansel to fill his pockets with white stones. So he did. And all along the way we dropped white stones. That night, when the moon shone bright, we followed the white stones back home." Gretel has spied a basket of onions in the corner. She takes one and peels.

"You should have seen the look on the witch's face when we showed up the next morning," says Hansel.

"Please, please," I say, "don't call her a witch. Just call her your evil stepmother." And I am already wondering if this woman, so maligned, is truly a witch. But a witch would have more effective ways of disposing of unwanted children. So she is just one more wayward soul. I wonder what mistake she made, what crime of the soul she committed, to bring herself to the state of mercilessness that these children speak of.

"But the next afternoon when she sent us away again," says Gretel, now chopping the onion with my only knife, "stupid Hansel here—"

"I'm *not* stupid."

"He puts bread crumbs in his pockets instead of stones."

"It takes time to gather that many stones," says Hansel. His eyes water from the onion. I smile. This one is no use in the kitchen at all. I pull my small hand towel off the bowl of rising bread dough near the hearth and hand it to him. He dabs his eyes and walks over to the window.

"So the birds ate the crumbs, of course," says Gretel. She wipes her hands on her skirt.

"You need an apron," I say, as I shape the bread dough and put it on a flat pan. I open the oven in my hearth and slide in the pan.

Gretel looks down at the stains on her skirt. "I've slept in this for three nights now. It doesn't matter how much dirtier it gets."

I nod. She is a practical girl.

"Where's the endive?" Gretel looks around the kitchen area as she talks.

"I have to cut it." I take the knife from her and leave, walking quickly through the late-afternoon rays. I can see the moon rising already. It is a full moon of the new month. I walk to the corner of my garden just inside the marigolds. Without the marigolds, all my endive would be eaten by the rabbits. But the smell of marigolds protects it.

I look at the marigolds as if I'm seeing them for the first time. They are cheerful and simple. I make a pocket of my skirt and fill it with endive. Then I cut two sprigs of marigold. I march back.

Gretel's shoes stand just inside the door. She is on her knees, helping Hansel take his off. She rises as I come in. I walk to her and weave a sprig of marigold into each of her braids.

"You will be a beautiful woman," I say.

"I'll settle for being good. Like you," says Gretel.

I want to smile at her no-nonsense attitude. It is a pity

she didn't have a beauty-loving mother like mine to soften her core, to open her to the pleasure around her.

Gretel walks to the window and catches the reflection of herself in the spun-sugar glass. "Still, flowers are a treat now and then." She smiles and returns to the table.

I want to clap my hands with happiness at the evidence that this child is not yet so bound by her pastor's strict warnings that she cannot enjoy beauty. But I don't clap. She might think my happiness trivializes her efforts to be pious. I won't risk alienating this fine child. She is working again already. I nod silently.

She soaks the endive in the water bucket. "And the chicken?"

Fear tightens its grip on my chest. "I have no meat."

Gretel looks at me solemnly. "We got very poor in the last year. We had only what meat we could hunt. You are an old woman. You cannot be a good hunter." She lifts her chin proudly. "Poverty and age are nothing to be ashamed of. We will use much garlic." She takes fresh garlic from her pocket. "I found it in the woods. We've been chewing on it, to keep the evil spirits at bay."

"And fennel, too," says Hansel, holding up a limp stalk. "Mother said fennel helps in the night battles against the devils."

I step back automatically. I have seen both plants growing wild in these southern woods. I have stepped around them with care. "Add the garlic and fennel to your own bowls once they are on the table. I am neither a garlic eater nor a fennel eater." Then I move closer to Gretel and put my fingers on her cheek. "You are not just lovely to look at," I say, "you are clever."

"I'm clever, too," says Hansel.

"That remains to be seen," says Gretel.

"Don't be hard on your brother," I find myself saying, although I, too, don't know if this boy is clever.

"Our mother always said that," says Gretel, looking at me with guileless eyes. She smashes the garlic expertly and puts it on a plate on the table. She looks around. "Where are the hot pads?"

"Hot pads?" I say, feeling a small panic. I must be careful not to betray myself. I have been inured to the pain of heat ever since my brief hours as the salamander of vermillion in that birch grove those nine long years ago. Fire can eat my flesh, but it causes me no pain. I have no need of hot pads.

"I have to hang the soup pot on the hook in the fireplace."

"But the pot isn't hot yet," I say, stupidly.

"Of course it's not hot," says Gretel, looking at me

curiously. "But the hook is hot. What if I touch it? Where are the hot pads?"

"Here," I say, picking up an old towel from the small stack by the wall. "You can use this."

Gretel takes the towel from me with a doubtful face. She sets the pot on the hook in the fireplace. Then she turns to me with a face bright from the heat of the fire. "Tomorrow we can catch a rabbit." She smiles faintly. "I'm very good with a slingshot. There are not many foods better than roast rabbit."

I give no answer. An answer will come to me in time, I know. For now, the danger is not immediate. I can let the child's words pass.

We eat endive soup in quiet peace. I am careful to take the bread from the oven with the old towel, rather than my bare hands. The smell of the fresh bread is almost as good as its taste. The children eat ravenously. And soon even Hansel is washing up with us and sweeping and wiping the table.

The children are hiding yawns. I smile at their innocent politeness. "You must climb into bed now. Hurry and strip."

Gretel shakes her head. "We've been sleeping in the woods and . . . and we've come to prefer the feeling of leaves underneath us."

"We have not," shouts Hansel.

"Yes, we have," says Gretel firmly. "I'll carry in some leaf piles and we'll sleep in the corner."

I am shocked, almost hurt. "Is there something wrong with the bed?"

"There's nothing wrong with the bed," shouts Hansel. "I'm sleeping in the bed."

"No, you're not," says Gretel. "There is only one bed. It is for the Old Woman."

I laugh. "Oh, Gretel, let me tell you a secret." I lean forward and whisper. "I never sleep. I will be just as comfortable in the rocking chair all night."

"You never sleep?" says Hansel, his eyes growing round.

"Never," I say.

"Why not?" says Hansel.

"Don't be nosy," says Gretel, but her eyes are as round as his.

I am charmed by her protective behavior toward my privacy. It moves me to speak openly. "I am afraid of what may come to me in my sleep."

Gretel stares at me.

"Our father had nightmares," says Hansel.

"Yes," I say to the boy, "nightmares. Many people suffer from nightmares." I smile kindly. "To bed now."

The children strip and climb into the rough cotton sheets I have woven myself.

"That bowl," says Gretel, pointing, "did you make it?"

"Yes."

She looks at the bowl with a flicker of longing. But the words that come out do not betray her desire. "It is a good size. It could have many uses."

"I keep it empty," I am saying. "I keep it pure."

Gretel's face lights up. "Yes, it looks pure."

"Do you think it's pretty?" I ask.

"Pretty? I suppose it is," says Gretel thoughtfully. "But it is pure. That's what counts."

"Tomorrow," I am saying, "tomorrow I will make a fresh batch of caramels." I am thinking that I would love to feed this girl chocolate—the rich milk chocolate that Asa loved so much. But cacao beans are impossible to come by without going into a village store. Even making caramels means I must lure a farmer's cow away from the herd so I can rob her of a bucket of milk. Almost nothing is without its risks. But I need to make Gretel candy. "Would you like fresh caramels?"

Gretel doesn't answer, nor does Hansel; both children sleep already.

I quickly boil a vat of water. I collect their clothes and empty their pockets. I set Gretel's wishbone on the table beside the pile of odd sticks and beetle shells from Hansel's pockets. I throw the clothes into the boiling water with peppermint leaves. After a while, I lift them out. I realize I am holding these scalding hot clothes in my bare hands. I look quickly over my shoulder to make sure the children have not seen. They are fast asleep. I must learn to be careful. I wring out the children's clean clothes and hang them on a grapevine cord across the room.

Then I grab my broom and search carefully in every nook and cranny. I find a potato bug that must have traveled in with the last batch of beets. I take no chances, but throw it into the boiling vat. I find some ants, dining on crumbs from our dinner bread. I crush them. There are no other living creatures on the floor. Nevertheless, I open my jug of vinegar and splash the floor liberally. I get on hands and knees and rub the pungent acid into every floorboard.

My eyes scour the walls now. Nothing.

The ceiling. Nothing.

But, oh, what was that? I move closer. The delicate leg of a hairy spider protrudes from a niche between the logs near the ceiling. If I smash with the broom, the spider may pull itself entirely into the niche and escape. And who knows what powers that spider may answer to? I must entice the creature from the niche. I walk calmly to the hearth and set down my broom. So long as no devil knows that these children are here, so long as no devil can speak within my head, these children may live here with me. I can take care of them. I have lived in isolation for nine long years. Surely it is time for me to have companionship again. We can be a family of sorts. After all, their stepmother is cruel beyond belief and their father is an obvious coward. They can't be worse off with me. They can't, so long as the devils do not know they are here. I must face that spider. If it has furious eyes, I must kill it.

I walk quietly to the wall below the niche where the spider hides. I get down on my hands and knees and examine the floor. I buzz lightly, like the sound of a fly in distress. I buzz on and on. I dare not look up at the wall. I buzz and keep my head lowered so that nothing above my head can see the source of the buzz. I buzz on and on. I can hear the spider's breath-soft steps on the wall. It is a female spider. I sense her femininity. She is very close now. Her eyes burn into the nape of my neck.

I grab her with one swift move and gnash her between my teeth. I hesitate; then I spit her out. She is gone, like a whiff of dust. My tongue licks the bitter ash of instant death from my teeth.

eight

Jewels

The children are asleep in my bed. I stand over them and feel their breath curl around their cheeks. I marvel at the contrast of their dark lashes on their pink skin. I brush Gretel's hair away from her temple, as I once did to Asa's hair. I slide my index finger into a ring of Hansel's hair. It is the first ring of sorts that I have had on my finger since that fateful ring of Spanish gold. Such a difference between the two rings. I blow Hansel's ringlet off my finger. They are gentle children.

We have been living together here for four weeks. I know this by the cycle of moons. We are now back to a full moon. The children have adjusted quickly to a vegetarian diet, though they spoke at first of meat. I told them that my religion forbids me to swallow flesh. They believe me. It is not far from the truth.

I am interested to learn that I can answer questions without being deceitful. Indeed, I have never yet lied to these children. I simply present only what they need to know. The rest is left hidden, hurting no one. That my answers are measured and not free does not render them knavish. Always have I understood perspective. Was it not this same perspective I employed so long ago when I responded to Bala's questions about Asa's father?

I am standing looking at my own hands. They have changed in the last month. They are covered with callouses from gripping the broom. I sweep our home many times each day, and when I sweep I hold on to that broom with a passion I can barely control. The skin around my nails peels back from the acid of the vinegar I pour generously on the shelves three times each day. There is not a single insect in this home. Not a single spider. This is a clean home, a home free of devils, a home fit for children.

I step back and crush a pinecone Hansel has left on the floor. I jump at the sound. Hansel is making a wreath for the door, but this cone will not be part of it. The noise disturbs Gretel's sleep. She looks around in momentary alarm. Then her eyes focus on my face and they become dreamy. She smiles. "Good night, Mother." She closes her eyes and is instantly deep asleep.

I have stopped breathing. Now I let the air fill my lungs once more. This child has called me Mother. My ears are ringing with the word. It is an unexpected honor.

I walk backward slowly and lower myself into the rocking chair, feeling dazed. I look about the one-room cottage, as Gretel has taught me to call it. Gretel's apron, which took me four days to make, is folded on the shelf above the bed. Ordinarily I could pick the cotton, spin it, and weave it all within a single day. But the apron is not plain cotton. The edges are scalloped with crochet. I have dyed the loops pink. I smile at the pervasive signs of beets in this home. There are bunches of dried currants sewn above the pockets. They give a festive air to the little apron. When the currants begin to turn to dust, I will replace them. The supply of dried berries is without end.

Beside the apron on the shelf sits a small stack of hot pads. Gretel made them, in her quiet, insistent way. She never questioned me further about them. I have much to be grateful for.

And beside the stack of hot pads is my carved wooden bowl. It is still empty. But its significance has changed.

I have promised Gretel that when I die, it is hers. I know what this promise means: I have accepted Gretel as a daughter. And now, oh, joy of joys, she has called me Mother. We have adopted each other.

She is a very different girl from the girl Asa was. Gretel is made of oak, where Asa was a bending willow. Gretel would smell of soap, where Asa would prefer perfume. But, after all, I am a very different woman today from the woman I was when I was Asa's mother. Gretel is a more suitable child to the woman I am now. She doesn't demand I give the warmth only a human can give. I give all that I can, and it seems enough. Gretel is satisfied with me. I feel a calm I had never expected to feel again.

Peeking out from under the edge of the bed is a new basket that Hansel made. It is crude and asymmetrical. But I like it. It is now full of feathers from the head and tail of the redheaded woodpecker. Hansel is quite expert at spying feathers. He would soar like a feather if he could. I have taken lately to holding his hand when we walk in the woods. Half the time he is breaking free from me to climb a tree for a feather stuck high in the branches. He has the same affinity for heights that Asa had. But he always returns quickly and takes my hand again. Feathers. I think briefly of the basket of feathers that Asa kept in our cabin long ago. I picture the delight her face would show at the sight of the bright yellow feathers of these birds that call themselves canaries.

Fine, fine children. Both of them. Children who deserve so much.

And I am standing now, walking to the hearth. I am reaching my hands into the ashes, which are still smoldering. I do not look over my shoulder to check whether or not the children watch. Their even breaths tell me they sleep peacefully. I clear away the ashes and dig with my bare fingers into the baked clay earth. It takes most of an hour, but my fingers at last feel the sharp edges of the porcupine-quill box. It is still whole, after these nine long years of being buried. I unearth it and set it beside my knees. Then I fill the hole and push the ashes back in place.

I look at my sizzling skin. Scars will form. I plunge my hands into the bucket of water that sits beside the hearth. It would make no sense to let the burn eat to the bone.

I get to my feet and look at the dirt-covered box. I can already imagine the emeralds in a necklace lying on Gretel's thin chest. I look at her shoes by the door. Her feet are small. I am sure I have enough diamonds for the soles of her shoes. But no one would rob her here in the woods.

I could cover her shoes with diamonds, top and bottom. Asa would have laughed in glee had it been safe to stud the tops of her shoes in diamonds. Gretel will be more hesitant. I will have to help her learn to let herself enjoy the splendor.

I go out into the night. The air is chilled. Summer is coming to a close with the end of August, and I can smell that this will be a harsh winter. I think of Hansel and Gretel's stepmother, looking ahead to a hard winter, wondering how she would feed these children. That must have been it. No woman would abandon these children for anything less than desperation.

And I wonder why I want to justify her actions so much. Who is this wicked stepmother to me and me to her?

But it is not her I care about. It is the children. I seek to justify her actions so that I can quell the rage that lights within me at the thought of her cruelty.

But, oh, joyous, milky-full moon up there in the sky, you witnessed the girl child's words tonight. I have no need for rage any longer. A new life has come to me. A new world.

And I realize suddenly that this is the second full moon this month. A blue moon. What is happening to me can happen only once in a blue moon.

I am running now, my feet knowing the way perfectly. My hands dip into the stream and wash the newly scarred skin to perfect cleanliness. I laugh a perfect laugh. There is nothing missing. I am very close to hope, after years and years of hopelessness. I cannot wait to get back and begin my work as jeweler. I run as fast as I have ever run. As fast as I crossed forests and lakes to get to these woods nine years ago.

I open the door and stop. My mouth drops open.

"Look!" Gretel is kneeling before the open porcupine box. Her hands are full of gems.

"What woke you?" My eyes race around the room. "What woke you, Gretel?"

"Nothing at all," says Gretel. She holds the gems close to her face. "Where did they come from?"

"What woke you?" I shriek.

Hansel sits up and rubs the sleep from his eyes.

"Nothing," says Gretel, surprise in her voice. "A silly spider on my cheek. Less than nothing."

Hansel is out of bed now, walking toward Gretel on bare feet.

"Where is that spider?" I hurry to the bed and stare down at the pillow, which still holds the indentation from her head.

"Why, I put it out the door. Its abdomen was brown,

not colored. It wasn't a poisonous one." Gretel laughs. "How can you think of a spider at a time like this? Just look, we are rich."

"We won't have to live in the woods anymore," says Hansel. He holds a ruby in his palm.

"That's right," says Gretel. "We can go back to town. We can bring enough jewels to make Father rich forever."

"They're leaving you," says the voice within my head.

The room spins before my eyes, and I fall into the rocking chair. I am shocked at the return of the voice. But the shock is momentary, for the words it speaks cut me so deeply I cannot retreat into a state of shock. I want to say that they are not leaving me. They talk of their father now. But that's just because the jewels are a novelty. As soon as they have a moment to think about it, they will remember me. They will talk about taking me with them.

"I'm going to make a belt and put this one on the buckle," says Hansel, pocketing the ruby.

"Don't be ridiculous," says Gretel. "It's worth money, you foolish boy. We can eat for a year on what this ruby is worth. Father can buy beef again." She takes the ruby from Hansel and puts it back in the box. She picks up a smaller one. "Here." She laughs. "Take this one for your buckle."

"You thought they loved you, didn't you?" The voice

within my head laughs raucously. "Imagine that, human children loving a witch! You pathetic piece of boar dropping!" And now a second voice breaks into laughter. "They will take all your jewels and leave you here alone. You thought love could save you. Watch. Watch it all crumble away! No one will love you ever ever again."

My hands clutch the arms of the rocking chair. I feel I am falling, despite my grip. I hold on with all my strength. The children are not talking about me. They are not planning to take me with them. But that's all right, I hasten to tell myself. That's the way it must be. It would be tragic if they wanted me to go with them, for I can never leave this enchanted forest. They are right. I am not hurt at their behavior. I will not be hurt.

"Of course you're hurt," says that demonic voice. "You are a disgrace to all witches everywhere. Pull yourself together. There they are—delicious morsels of meat."

"Look at this purple one," says Gretel. She holds up the amethyst I used to draw magic circles with.

I do not look at Gretel's pink flesh. I concentrate on the amethyst. I cannot think how it came to be in the box. I used it with the baron's newborn that day nine years ago. But then it was left in the dirt. Who rescued it? And now I am sure it was Asa. And knowledge of

Asa floods my mind. I see her kissing the amethyst nine years ago and setting it in the porcupine box all shiny wet with her tears. And I see her now. This very moment. I see her swirling skirts. I fight the knowledge. It comes to me from an unclean source. I would give anything to know about Asa, anything but the right to resist killing these two children here. I am fighting and fighting.

Gretel comes to the chair and stands beside me, her eyes worried. "Are you all right? You don't look good."

"She never looks good," said Hansel. "She's a hunchback. You told me it didn't matter whether she looked good, so long as she was good."

"Hush, Hansel." Gretel puts her hand on top of mine. "Are you ill?"

"Tell her," scream the voices in my head. "Tell Gretel what ails you. Watch the hate that comes into her eyes! Tell her, tell her, tell her."

My tongue moves of its own accord. "Gretel," I whisper. All my strength is unable to stop my tongue. "Gretel."

Her hand tightens over mine. "What is it? You are making me afraid."

I will never tell Gretel the hideous words that hide behind my lips. I reach my hand into my mouth and grab my tongue. I pull it forward, and my teeth clamp down hard. My tongue flies away across the room, wagging as it goes. I swoon.

When I awake, the voices are frantic. "Open your eyes! Open them."

I place the index finger of each hand on each eyelid and hold it there. My eyelids freeze shut.

"You wretched fool!" The voice within me splutters now. "You think you can close your mind by not seeing the fresh meat before you. Imbecile. You know they are here. You know the blood that runs through their veins. You can smell it. You can taste it! Your self-imposed blindness is futile. No matter what you do, you know they are here—in the flesh and blood."

My ears listen against my will. I hear sniffles.

"Don't cry, Gretel," says Hansel.

"I'm not crying." Gretel sniffles loudly.

I hear clinking noises.

"Yes, you are. Don't cry. The Old Woman will be all right. Look, her tongue is still alive."

"Get away from that thing and stuff your pockets," hisses Gretel.

"It's still moving," says Hansel. "It wants me to cup it in my hands so it can speak."

"Don't touch it!" I hear a slap. "Listen to me, Hansel. Did you see any blood when she bit her tongue off?"

"You hurt me. Don't hit me, or I'll wake her up and tell her. She always says you have to be nice to me."

"Don't be daft, Hansel. Blood. There was no blood."

"No blood," says Hansel.

"That can mean only one thing," says Gretel.

"What?" says Hansel.

"That she's a witch, you idiot."

"A witch!" Hansel whispers now. "A witch?"

"Fill your pockets with jewels. We're leaving."

"But we don't know which way to go."

"It doesn't matter which way we go," says Gretel. "If we stay here, we're doomed."

Their footsteps pass my chair.

"Listen!" says the voice in my head. "Listen to love lost." The voice laughs. "Do what you must!"

I am rising quickly. My eyes are still frozen shut, but I move without stumbling. My hands reach for the wooden bar. I hear the clank as it drops across the door in front of the children. They are locked in. I have imprisoned them. I know precisely where they are, despite my frozen-shut eyes. My mouth opens in anticipation. I fight myself. I don't want to be walking toward them. I don't want to. But I cannot stop my feet.

"Eat them," scream the voices in my head. There are many voices now. "Eat them, eat them, eat them."

nine

The Magic Circle

Hansel sits in the cage I built slowly but expertly, despite my blindness. It hangs from the ceiling beam. I know he is sitting because I heard him plop down five minutes ago. He alternates between begging to be let out and working on his wreath. I have put the pine boughs and cones in with him to keep him quiet. I cannot risk hearing him cry. I cannot risk letting the devils see how I react to his tears.

"Why must I sweep again?" says Gretel. I touch her shoulder lightly, and she shudders with revulsion. I know she is leaning over her broom. She is very, very tired. "I have swept this room a dozen times already. I have wiped with the vinegar-soaked rag in every corner. This room is clean, I swear to you. It is clean."

I cannot tell her what I want that broom to do in her hands. I can no longer speak, of course. But more than that, I cannot allow myself to think through the details of the plan I know is forming deep within me. I am ever watchful of the voices that fill my head. They seem to know only part of my thoughts. If I am careful, who knows what may happen. It is two days since I unearthed the box. For two days these children have been alive on stolen time. Stolen from the devils. I have stumbled about most of this time. But whenever I have performed some act the devils believe will lead to the end they want, I have moved freely in my blindness, with no hesitation whatsoever. It is as though they steer me in these acts. I worked methodically, with painstaking care, on Hansel's cage—and they allowed me each long hour. Now I tap Gretel's broom insistently, and she sweeps once more. The devils do nothing to stop her. Perhaps they think I make her labor as a form of punishment. Or perhaps they know her sweeping is futile.

"How did it happen like this?" says Gretel, more to herself than to me. She has asked this question repeatedly over the past two days. "What changed everything?" And now I know her tone will change. It always does at this point. Her voice becomes reed-thin. She is no longer a girl of steel. She is the most fragile of children. "I hate jewels. I hate everything beautiful to the eye." Now she will stamp her foot. But, no, she does not. Instead, she adds something I have not heard her say before. "There is something very wrong here. You were not a witch when we first came. You loved us, I know." Her voice resonates like the most sacred of church bells. It is all at once womanly. I know she has arrived at a new perspective. I know she will never be a child again. She no longer pleads. All hope has been abandoned. She admits the reality of the evil she has seen. Would that I could grieve for her. She is as hopeless now as Peter was when first I met him. "Oh, wild and mysterious world," intones the child-woman Gretel, "if I had the power, I would strike all humans blind."

I am standing unmoving through these words, mesmerized, wanting them to go on forever. Wanting Gretel to understand all of it. But when she comes to her final statement, her desire to strike all humans blind, I jerk myself to attention. It is a daring statement. She speaks of what she would do if she had destructive powers. I wonder if Gretel realizes her dare. Is she trying to provoke the powers that be? Does she invite the devils to propose a pact? Oh, ignorant child. How thoughtlessly we tread, how easily we stumble. This child cannot fall prey to them. She must not.

I listen hard. The devils are not provoked. I hear no response from them. They ignore her in their unwavering focus on me. My evil protects the girl, an irony I value. I would take Gretel into my arms and console her if I were allowed a response myself. But no indulgences can I permit myself now. Besides, she would only shudder again at my touch.

I walk to Hansel's cage and tap the boy's knee, which always sticks out of the cage at a certain angle. "Hhhhhh," I force from my throat.

Hansel understands the crude order. He extends the half of the chicken wishbone that Gretel used to carry in her pocket. These children think I do not know it is the bone. They think that with my eyes sealed I know very little. I touch the bone between thumb and index finger.

"How does my finger feel?" says Hansel in a tired voice.

I touch the bone again and think in clear words: The boy is still too thin to eat. His finger has no flesh on it. He's nothing but skin and bones. I repeat the thought, loudly, if thoughts can be loud.

I have bargained with the many devils that speak in my head—so many that I cannot identify them all. One of them has emerged as a spokesman. That one has agreed: Gretel will go free. Yes, she may yet perish, alone in the woods, once she has left me. But at least she will have a chance. In payment, I will eat Hansel.

I play the game in my head. I repeat that I will eat Hansel. The demons must not know that this is a game. They must believe it.

I lean back in the rocking chair.

"A game?" The voice that has been silent for two days mocks me. "Do you really think you're fooling anyone? Oh, you mindless peasant midwife! You never learn. You think you've struck a bargain with us." There is much laughter in my head. "You think you'll outwit us and break your end of the bargain." The laughter is hysterical now. "You numskull! We won't be fooled a second time. You bargained for Asa's life; then you hid. You have done not one single stitch of work for the devils yet. You ingrate! But you are about to repay us, at last." The voice stops for a moment. I swallow the hard lump in my throat. The voice chuckles. "What a miracle your ignorance is! Once you taste Hansel's blood, it is all over. The struggle will be done. And you will gladly grab that girl whose hair you decorate with flowers; you will grab her and fry her with salt and a dash of paprika!"

I hold my hands on the sides of my head and try to pull my own head off my neck as the laughter deafens me.

"And then you will go to the nearest town," says the voice. "You will eat whatever children you meet. We will keep you hungry for blood for nine years. You had nine years as a sorceress, making us jump at your ridiculous orders. Then for nine years you cheated us, hiding here in the woods. You will now repay in full. Three cycles of nine years, and the last will be the best. Every single child you pass will perish."

I can taste the hot, sweet blood in my mouth. The blood of infants. It is flawlessly delicious.

This is it. I have lost. They know my thoughts, my plans. They know everything. And knowledge gives them power. They control my deepest desires. I am doomed to eternal torment. There is no solution. I am at last like Gretel as she spoke just a moment ago: I admit the evil that is.

But no! No, Gretel must not admit it. I am old and lost. But the girl must not be lost. She has a right to hope. She is innocent and good. I owe her that right. I must restore it for her. I must hope for her. Dare I entertain a hope? Me, who has gone so long utterly hopeless? But even a lost soul deserves a hope. Hope is the final refuge. Can devils hear hopes?

I stand up suddenly. I lean over the fire in the hearth, and my eyelids unfreeze. My eyes focus instantly and find the corner where my tongue lies, unmolested by the children. Gretel has obviously been careful to sweep around it. I walk to my tongue and replace it in my mouth.

The girl gasps.

"Asa, light the fire in the oven."

"Asa? Who is Asa? I am Gretel."

Hansel stands up and holds on to the bars of the cage.

"Asa, Gretel, what difference does it make? Light the fire." I stalk around the room, frantic. "I will eat your brother now."

Hansel screams and collapses on the bottom of the cage.

Gretel opens the oven door and throws in wood. She lights it from the fire that burns slowly in the hearth. She is crying as she works.

I open the porcupine-quill box. "Gretel, take these diamonds." I pick them out one by one. I am not thinking. I am only doing. I must not think. Hopes need not be thought.

Gretel watches me without moving from in front of

the oven. Her face shows revulsion at the sight of the diamonds.

I go to the door and pick up one of her shoes. I hold a diamond to the sole. It sticks fast. I pour the other diamonds that I hold in my skirt into her shoes.

"Do you love pretty things, Gretel?"

Gretel shakes her head in confusion. She knows I have just heard her say she hates beautiful things.

"Then why were you trying to steal my jewels?"

"Other people like pretty things," says Gretel. Her face is wary. She looks as though she expects me to burst into a tantrum.

"Go on," I am saying.

"I would have sold the jewels to others so that my family could eat and live decently."

I knew her answer before she spoke, of course. But I needed to hear her words. I needed to get her to speak of her family. "Your family," I say. "Your cursed stepmother tried to get you killed."

"Our father loves us."

"Your father let her send you into the woods to die," I say.

"He was weak," says Gretel. "He is suffering now. I know he must be suffering."

"How can you forgive him?" I ask.

"What choice do I have?" says Gretel. "We must have pity on the weak."

"You and Hansel were weak," I say, "and he had no pity on you."

"He loves me," says Gretel. "He loves Hansel. In the end, that's all that matters. Forgiveness is a little thing when love is there."

My skin prickles at the word. "Love," I say. "Gretel, could you . . ." My voice catches in my throat. "Could you forgive me?" I whisper.

"If you eat Hansel," Gretel is saying, placing one glittering word after the other into the air between us, her eyes shimmering, "I will . . ." And now she cannot hold back the hysteria that speaks through her eyes. It bursts from her mouth. She cries and screams, "If you eat Hansel, I will never forgive you!"

I search wildly through the jewels in the box. I grab at the amethyst. A spark shoots through my body. "Blessed amethyst!" I cry out, dropping it. "I cannot touch holy things. I cannot touch your holiness. I cannot touch my blessed amethyst." I wring my empty hands. I gnash my iron teeth. I speak in a harsh voice. "Is the fire hot enough yet, Gretel?"

She looks at me as though I've lost my senses. She is

shaking. She chews on the fat part of her palm. I know she is working to catch hold of herself once more. "Hot enough?" She seems barely able to process the words.

"Is it hot enough, girl?"

She jumps at my shout. She blinks. She is mastering the hysteria now. Rationality returns to her eyes. Or a semblance of rationality. "Hot enough?"

"Yes. I want you to check it. It must be just the right heat. It has to be perfect." I stare at her, willing her with my eyes to understand. This girl understands so much. She must understand just one last thing. She is rational again now. She must understand. "The fire has to be perfect."

Gretel's eyes hide the beginnings of a thought. She looks in the oven. "I don't know. I don't know how hot the fire must be to roast a human."

I nod my head in agreement, wondering if I really saw some glimmer of understanding in her or if that was just my hopes fooling me. I wish I could give some sign to her now. But they might see. "You stupid human," I say roughly. "Must I test it for myself?"

"Yes," whispers Gretel. "Test it yourself."

I walk to the shelf and take down the carved wooden bowl she loves so much. I turn and look her straight in the eye.

She stares at me, unblinking, almost not breathing.

I walk to Gretel and hold out the bowl. She makes no move to take it. There is tragedy in her face. I place the bowl at her feet. She opens her mouth as if to speak, but I touch my finger to her lips and hold it there, until her lips are so cold and numb, she will not be able to speak for several minutes. Her eyes are luminous and wet. They call to me. I dare not answer their call.

I open the oven door and lean in. The noise of the fire is a symphony to my ear. I count the tongues of the flames to pass the time. What is keeping the child? I lean in farther.

"What are you doing?" asks the voice in my head.

I lean farther into the oven. I must not think about the devil's question. I must hear only the loud fire. The heat is palpable. My face and chest part it with effort.

"What are you doing?" The voice within me is angry. "Your body can burn, mindless witch! Don't be fooled by the lack of pain. Beware! Do not lean any farther."

I empty my mind. Farther. I lean farther. I am almost crawling into the oven. Each second drags. I wait and wait. How long can I keep my mind empty? My eyelashes scorch.

And now I feel a tug at my cloak. Is the child trying to pull me back? Has she failed to comprehend, after all?

I shrug her off brusquely. The girl persists. I put my hand back, and my fingers close over Gretel's fingers. Hers slip away instantly, and I am clutching my rough cloak circled around a lump. I do not know what it is, but I can feel it strain to fly from me. I hold tight; my grip is iron.

Gretel pushes me in at last, strong and efficient. She shuts the door behind me with a sacred slam.

"Change!" screams the voice in my head. "Change into the salamander of vermillion! Change, you stupid, cowering midwife."

The heat, true to form, brings me no pain. I watch as my skirt and blouse catch fire. The lambent flames dance across my body. They lick my hair into flickers of light.

"You are damned! Don't you dare burn up! Change into the salamander! Change right now!"

I can hear Gretel screaming in the kitchen. She is screaming and screaming. Her cry is: "Mother!"

I pull the lump from where the folds of my skirt have turned to ash. The amethyst glows rich, royal purple. It no longer resists my touch. I draw a magic circle around myself with this final gift from the girl child. Then I raise the amethyst to my cheek. A tear glistens on the gem, then sizzles into steam. It was my own tear. Oh, miracle tear!

I can cry. And now I am crying for joy. Hallowed be hope, after all. I am crying with rapture. I am dying. Dying into the waiting hands of God.

I am dying.

Oh, glorious death.

I am dying.

Dying.

Free.